THE MATTER OF A MISPLACED DOCUMENT

A HADLEY SISTERS MYSTERY

BY

Elizabeth A. Martina

SERRA BOOKS, AN IMPRINT OF

Lanternarius Press

This story is a wholly imaginative work and, even if it contains references to real people, living or dead, the work is not meant to be a true story. Any similarities to real people are sheer coincidence.

Published by Lanternarius Press,

Oriskany, N.Y.

DEDICATION

To my ever-patient husband, Bob, who listens to
my disjointed storylines and lends an ear when I
get stuck in my writings. I can only do this
because of you!

SATURDAY AFTERNOON

"Ladies and gentlemen, please gather around the dais. The bidding is beginning in two minutes." The crowd slowly quieted down and took seats in front of the raised platform where a large table stood. On it were several dozen large paper bags, well filled with white tissue-paper wrapped items.

"The purpose, as you know, is to raise funds to complete the last payment for the design and installation of the organ, which our church began three years ago." The speaker, a petite brunette dressed in a tailored grey suit, was interrupted by a round of polite applause. She smiled and went on. "Understanding this, we hope that you will be most generous in your bids. Our auctioneer for this afternoon is the organizer of this white elephant sale, and my sister, Elizabeth Hadley. Please welcome her to the podium." Katherine Hadley backed away from the podium, joining in the applause, and smiled as Betty stepped up.

Small, with blonde curls pulled back in a wrap, in the newest fashion, Betty looked professional in a navy-blue suit and coordinating hat and shoes. Her self-confidence permeated the room as she looked out at the seventy or so people collected, people she had grown up around. Taking a deep breath, she began.

"Here we have our first bag of goods, each item wrapped

individually in tissue paper and cardboard so that it is difficult to identify. After all, that is the whole purpose of the wrappings," she smiled. Lifting up the bag closest to her, she noted, "It is about ten pounds." She shook it gently. "And no loose parts. How much can we start with? Ten dollars?"

A man raised his hand. "I bid $10."

The bidding was off to a good start and within two minutes, the church had collected $23.

Betty was able to maintain interest through the next 32 bags until they were all sold. The polite applause was short as the audience began collecting their bags of unknown contents. Betty took a sip from her water glass and sighed. Kate finished handing out the last of the bags and smiled at her sister.

"Our treasurer has tallied $727! Isn't that amazing for other people's second hand items? With Dad offering to round up to the nearest $100, we have $800 for Mr. Harrison's final bill. What a relief to have that expense off the shoulders of the vestry."

The custodian, John, walked in from the kitchen, wiping his hands on a towel. "That is all clean, Miss Hadley. Why don't you go? You have been here since 8 this morning. You must be tired. I can put away the chairs and tables."

"Thank you, John!' Betty looked at her watch. "Eight hours. No wonder I am tired!" She picked up her purse from within a storage cabinet and turned to Kate.

At that second, a long, piercing scream was heard from beyond the exterior door of the parish community building. It was loud enough that all those who were still in the room jumped in reaction. Then, most people dropped their bundles and raced for the exit. Kate and Betty, being more spry than most of the middle-aged and elderly people who attended, were first to reach the door and rushed through to the sidewalk. Two of the younger men from the audience were seen running down the street.

On the ground sat a middle-aged woman, hat askew, still screeching and red-faced. Sitting beside her was the bag she had just won at the auction, torn at the top and ripped at the bottom. Two still-wrapped items sat at a distance, on the grass. The sisters ran over to her and bent over, looking for injuries.

"What happened, Mrs. Stevens?" Kate asked, taking hold of the lady's elbow and hand. The woman stopped screeching when the friendly faces arrived, but she sobbed loudly. "Here, let's get up off the ground," Kate insisted. Betty got Mrs. Stevens' left side and they pulled her, huffing and puffing up to her feet. An older gentleman offered to walk her back into the community room while Betty picked up the bag and Kate chased after the loose items. By the time the girls got back to the room, Mrs. Stevens was seated on an upholstered chair and panting furiously.

Betty placed the ripped paper bag on an end table. It listed to the right. "I am going to have to get you a new bag to carry," Betty pointed out. Mrs. Stevens nodded as John handed her a glass of water. After a few sips, the woman began to calm down.

"You poor dear. Let me fix your hat and hair," Kate offered. Mrs. Stevens lips moved slightly, in an attempted smile. She nodded but said nothing.

"Can you tell us what happened?" Kate asked.

Mrs. Stevens looked at her. "Did the men get him?" she asked in a breathless voice.

Kate looked at her, puzzled. "Get who?"

"The young man who grabbed my bag! I wouldn't give it to him and when he finally pulled hard, I let go and it dropped to the sidewalk, spilling all over. Something broke. I heard it." Mrs. Stevens looked like she wanted to cry some more. Betty handed her a handkerchief, which the older lady used immediately. "He looked at me in surprise. I remember that! I don't know why he would be surprised. He didn't know what was in the bag any more than I do. And then he took off." She sniffed. "And those two brave men ran after him."

By this time, half of the people who had attended the auction were back inside, making sure their friend and neighbor was intact. They stayed to add their comments about the few seconds of excitement and disaster.

Kate and Betty looked at each other. Each knowing what the other was thinking.

"Let me inventory this bag for you, Mrs. Stevens. Let's see

what broke," Betty said as soothingly as possible. "Do you mind?"

"No, dear." Mrs. Stevens' voice had come back. "I am curious to know what he would have taken that could have been so important." She turned on the cushion to see the bag and its contents better.

Betty took the bag, put it on the floor and proceeded to take all the items out, one by one and put them on the end table. The one that fell to the bottom of the bag was the dish that had smashed.

"It is beyond repair, I am afraid," Betty said, looking at the ripped tissue paper, with porcelain fragments dropping as she pulled it out. Her nose wrinkled in disgust over the ruining of a perfectly useable painted dish. "Kate, please get my inventory list of bags from my purse." Betty stood holding what was left of the dish, pulling the tissue away.

Kate grabbed the list, referred to the number which corresponded to the number on the bag. "Luckily," she commented. "It is not an expensive piece. Just pretty."

Betty walked the tissue and porcelain over to the garbage and unceremoniously tossed it in. "Let's make sure that everything else is still here," she suggested, taking the list from her younger sister. She counted the remaining items and nodded. "All accounted for, Mrs. Stevens. Two books, some brass candlesticks, some serving flatware, a pen and ink, a set of embossed stationery."

Kate got out another paper bag and reloaded the still-wrapped items. By this time, Mrs. Stevens was feeling almost normal again. She stood up and smiled to the two young ladies.

"I thank you girls for helping me. At least, I didn't lose anything valuable." She sighed in relief.

"Do you think you would recognize that man again, if anyone catches him?" Kate asked, picking up the bag for the older lady.

"Oh, indeed I would! He was unusually short. And he had very pale eyes. Almost yellow. I have never seen eyes like that before," Mrs. Stevens admitted. "I surely would notice that if I ever saw them again."

Kate raised her eyebrows. "That is an unusual thing to notice. I will keep that in mind. You never saw him before?"

"No, never. I would have remembered." The woman nodded, accenting the comment.

"Can I offer you a ride home?" Betty asked.

"No, thank you. I just live just a few doors down on Mount Vernon."

"Never the less, I think you should be accompanied home," insisted the older gentleman who had walked her back in.

Mrs. Stevens, a widow, happily accepted the attentions of a gentleman.

SUNDAY EVENING

Kate and Betty returned from an evening coffee with their friends, Lt Detective Casey Roach and Detective Joe Talbot. They had told the men about the curious ending to the white elephant sale.

Kate was still unpinning her hat when the foyer phone rang. Thinking it was Casey, having forgotten something, she answered happily. "Hello, there!"

"Is this the Hadley residence?" came an unknown male voice.

Kate stood a little straighter. This was not a normal Sunday evening call. "Yes, it is. This is Katherine Hadley. How can I help you?"

"This is Mrs. Stevens' residence, Joseph speaking. Are you available to speak to Mrs. Stevens?"

"Certainly, Joseph. Is there any problem?"

"I am sure that Mrs. Stevens would prefer to speak to you, herself. One moment, please."

After thirty seconds, Mrs. Stevens came on the line. "Oh, Miss Hadley! I saw that man again!" The woman's voice trembled. "I didn't know who else to turn to!"

Kate took a deep breath. Betty came down the stairs and Kate signaled to her to pick up an extension. Betty flew back up to her room. When Kate heard the click, she continued.

"Which man? The one with the funny eyes from yesterday?"

"Yes, that's the one!"

"Where did you see him?"

"I went for a little walk, tonight. I have been so nervous about the incident yesterday that I couldn't concentrate on any of my radio programs. So, I thought I would just step out for a bit. I thought to walk as far as the church and back. And there he was, sitting on the front steps!"

"Oh, my! What did you do?" Kate leaned against the wall.

"I walked right back to the house and told Joseph. Then I decided to call you. What do you think I should do?"

"I do not think there is much you can do, Mrs. Stevens. But I know someone who can try to help. It is..." she looked at her watch. "It is 9:30. Let me try to contact him in the next half hour and ask him."

"Will you get back to me?" Mrs. Stevens sounded relieved that there was help.

"I can't promise tonight, but certainly tomorrow morning. If you are concerned, you do have your houseman there with you, correct?"

"Yes, and my cook. They are husband and wife. I had them so long that when my husband died, I couldn't stand to have them leave. Even though I really do not need them both, anymore."

"Good, then. Keep the doors locked and don't answer the door after 10. Keep an outside light on, for security purposes. I will call you when I have more information."

"That is very good of you, Miss Hadley. I look forward to hearing from you."

Kate bid the woman good night and ran upstairs to Betty's room. The impeccably kept room smelled of lavender and lilac, just like her sister.

"Do you see a pattern?" Kate asked as she burst unannounced into the room. Betty had hung up her extension and was pacing, a sign that she was deep in thought.

"I think we should call Joe and Casey. They will have some good ideas." Betty walked over to her phone on the bedside table. "Do you want to call or me?"

"You call. I will pick up in my room." Kate left and walked down the hall to her room. She threw her purse and hat on the bed and pushed a pile of books to the end of her chaise lounge so she could sit while they spoke. She picked up the receiver and joined in the conversation.

"So, this poor woman saw the same man today," Betty was saying.

"Maybe he just moved into the neighborhood," Joe suggested.

"People don't just move into this neighborhood, Joe," Betty objected. "It is a very stable one."

"You said she saw him this evening?" Casey asked. Kate could picture him taking notes.

"Yes. He was sitting on the steps of the church, like he was waiting for someone," Kate piped up.

"Certainly, you can't arrest someone for sitting on church steps, Kate."

"I know, but, in this neighborhood, what adult sits on steps of a church at 8 at night? This isn't Dorchester!" she sniffed. Kate immediately regretted saying that. Casey and Joe were from there. She bit her lip and decided to just listen.

"Did they speak?" Joe asked.

"Not that she told us," Betty responded. "And, yesterday, when he tried to grab the bag, he didn't say anything."

"So, no one knows what his voice sounds like." Casey concluded. "Can we get Mrs. Stevens to come in to make a report, maybe get a description?"

"Certainly, Casey. We will bring her in tomorrow morning!" Kate quickly said.

"Fine. I will see you, then."

MONDAY MORNING

Kate made the phone call to Mrs. Stevens' residence by 8:30 the next morning and left a message with the very concerned Joseph. She received a return call while on her second cup of coffee. Sally brought in the phone, with eyes twinkling, and placed it on the breakfast table. Kate reached for the receiver, winking at Sally at the same time. Sally had already been apprised of the situation.

"Good morning, Mrs. Stevens!" Kate began. "Can you come with me to the police precinct this morning? Lt Detective Roach would like to talk to you."

"Can he help solve this?"

"Well, he can help, if anyone can. I think there is something about the items you got in the bag. Can you bring them with you?"

The older woman hesitated. "I gave the bag to Joseph. I will ask him where that bag is." The phone was silent for at least 30 seconds. "I have the bag. It has not yet been emptied."

"We would like to take you down to the precinct office this morning."

"I never go anywhere by car unless Joseph is driving. I can pick you up at 10:30. Is that satisfactory?"

Kate eyebrows puckered on hearing that. Betty, half behind the newspaper, noted that and the throat clearing that followed. She put down her paper and looked at her sister, intently.

"That will be fine, Mrs. Stevens. We will be ready at 10:30."

Kate hung up the phone and turned to Betty. "We are taking Mrs. Stevens to talk to Casey this morning. When we spoke to the men last night, we sort of promised this and Casey sort of promised he would be around."

Betty smiled. "Yes, I think I heard you say something…"

"I had better call Casey and make sure." Kate grabbed the receiver and dialed the number of the downtown precinct. It was picked up after two rings.

"Good morning, Sgt. Ryan. This is Katherine Hadley. Is Lt Detective Roach available? … I will wait, thank you." She covered the mouthpiece and turned to Betty. "Casey is on another line." Thirty seconds later, she turned her attention back to the phone. "Good morning, Casey! I was hoping you had time this morning, about 11, to talk to our church friend who was knocked down on Saturday."

"I am working on a report and waiting for three people to call me back. If you can promise me that you will only be here for ten minutes, I can fit you in."

"That is wonderful, Casey!" Kate brightened. "Betty and I will bring Mrs. Stevens by just before 11! You are wonderful!" She hung up and turned to Betty. "It's almost 9:30. We had better get ready. He is only giving us ten minutes!"

"I will call James to bring the car around," Betty got up and went to the door.

"No. Mrs. Stevens will only be in a car where Joseph is the driver." Kate rolled her eyes. Betty's eyebrows went up and she stared for a moment, then shrugged her shoulders and headed for the stairs.

At 10:29, Joseph pulled up to the curb in front of the Hadley house. Mrs. Stevens was in the back seat. Betty took the front seat and Kate joined Mrs. Stevens in the back. It was mid-morning and the traffic was light going to the precinct office. After stopping to speak to Sgt Ryan, the girls accompanied the woman and her bag to Casey's office. He saw them standing at the door and motioned them in as he finished up a phone call. Kate made the introductions all around.

There were two chairs in the room. Casey moved his chair from behind his desk so all three visitors could sit. He perched on the edge of the desk.

"First, Mrs. Stevens, please explain what happened on Saturday afternoon," Casey began. The older woman, holding her gloved hands together tightly, explained in minute detail how she won the bag at the auction and carried her bag out the door, whereupon she was attacked.

"What happened to the man?"

"He ran off, chased by two of the male parishioners."

"But," Kate interjected. "They came back empty-handed."

Casey looked distressed. "And there was another time you saw him?"

"Yes!" she gushed. "Last night, I went for a walk just as it got dark. This whole thing had me so on nerve! And there he was. On the church steps, sitting, having a smoke. Just a few doors from my home!" Her right hand flew to her chest and her face reddened.

Casey got off the desk and bent down to pick up the bag that Mrs. Stevens had brought in. He set it on the desk and looked inside. The items were still wrapped in their white tissue paper. "You don't mind, do you, ma'am?" he asked holding up a wrapped book. She shook her head.

Kate and Betty leaned forward in their chairs as he carefully pulled the paper apart, looking for any hints. He laid the paper aside and looked at the book. "Charles Dickens' A Christmas Carol" he announced. "Good story. Older binding." He opened it to find the copyright date. Then he started flipping through the pages and a yellowed, obviously brittle, sheet fell out and fluttered to the floor. Kate bent over and picked it up. Still folded, she could see a corner of the sheet was ripped away and gone. She handed it back to Casey.

Unfolding the sheet, carefully, Casey read it silently and his eyes opened wide.

"What is it, Casey?"

He licked his lips and looked at Kate and then at Betty. "How much Massachusetts history do you know?"

"That was my most favorite subject in school," Betty said, putting her gloved hand out. "Let me see that." Casey very carefully handed her the sheet.

Betty looked at it for a minute. Stunned, she looked at Kate. "This looks like a will or a list of some sort. The writing is very faded. But I am sure that the name is Harvard."

"Harvard? John Harvard?" Kate asked.

Betty looked around the document. "I think that date is August? 1638?"

"How did that get into the book?" Kate asked no one in particular.

Mrs. Stevens, silent until now, stared at the paper. "That man was trying to steal that book!"

Casey stood up straight. "I have little doubt that this could be what the man was trying to get. But we are getting ahead of ourselves. First, I would like to know if this is an original, a copy from the time, or a fake." He put out his hand to take back the sheet. Betty reluctantly handed it back to him.

"I would like you ladies to go home. I will start an investigation, when I have some time, and I will start with that question. It will take a few weeks, with all the other work I have to do, but I will keep you apprised of all my findings." He handed the bag, and the rest of the unopened items, to Kate. "I am afraid that I have another appointment and I apologize for the small amount of time I could give you." He winked at Kate.

"Do I get that book and paper back?" the older woman asked.

"No. They are part of an investigation at this point. Here, let me write you out a receipt." Casey walked around his desk. He grabbed a pen from his drawer and two pieces of stationery which had "Boston Police Department" embossed on the top. He placed a sheet of carbon paper between the stationery and slipped them into the typewriter. He wrote a description of the items, only indicating a "Yellowed document-unidentified" and the book's title. "Here you go, Mrs. Stevens," he said, signing and folding it in half and handing it across the desk. She bobbed her head in acknowledgement and turned to leave.

Casey turned to Kate and kissed her forehead. "I will call you tonight," he whispered. She smiled up to him and followed Betty and the older woman out the door.

Back in the car, Mrs. Stevens was disappointed that she was not being protected from the man, whoever he was.

Kate reassured her. "Casey knows what he is doing. It is sometimes easier to find a person by finding what he needs rather than where he is. Does that make any sense?" Mrs. Stevens gloomily nodded in assent and was silent the rest of the short ride back to the Hadleys'. The sisters, on the other hand, were entranced with the new information and could barely keep quiet.

Over salmon loaf and Caesar salad, Betty and Kate had a chance to discuss this new piece of evidence.

"Casey isn't going to get to the list, or whatever it is, for weeks. He is so backlogged with, well, somewhat more important things to do," Kate commented.

"That leaves us free to help him out," Betty pointed out, sticking her fork into another piece of salmon loaf from the serving platter.

"I was just thinking about that, myself. What do you have in mind?" Kate put down her fork and gazed at her sister, ready to do whatever she suggested.

"The document may be historically valid or it may be a simple forgery. Being as this fellow who seems to be stalking Mrs. Stevens seems to be somehow related to the document..."

"We don't know that!"

"The timing is purely coincidental? I don't think so," Betty responded. "But, as I said, being as the two seem related, I think our first step is to track down someone who knows about old historical documents."

"You are brilliant!" Kate smiled. "Let's finish lunch and look up any historical agencies and old book retailers and get some information."

An hour later, the two were in their father's study reviewing the latest city directory. Kate had the heavy book on her father's desk and Betty sat, poised with pen and paper.

"Brattle Book Store is a good first choice." Kate commented as she reviewed the entries. "We are in there once a month as it is. I am sure Miss Baldwin or one of the other sales people can be of some help."

"And how about this?" Kate pointed to the name of the Massachusetts Historical Society. She gave Betty the information. "Miss Baldwin will probably tell us if it is the place to go."

Betty looked up after writing the address. "I bet we can do both of these this afternoon. We will just go in asking questions, not showing the document and then get Casey to give it to us to show them."

"I wonder if Casey will give it to us. It is evidence in a crime, after all," Kate pointed out. "We will, probably, have to have Casey come with it." She smiled conspiratorially as she closed the heavy directory and put it back on the shelf.

After getting hats, gloves and purses off the foyer buffet, the two sisters got into their Mercedes Benz roadster and took off down Charles St. to Beacon, followed the streets around the Common then turned onto West St. Betty found a parking spot right across from the little store and they went in.

A used bookstore smells like old paper, glue and tobacco with a slight tinge of mold. There is no other place that gets close to that sort of smell. Add to that hanging lights that cast shadows and it is almost like a scene from a mystery movie, itself. The Hadley sisters loved this place.

The moment they walked in, one of the sales managers, Irene Baldwin, walked up to greet them. She always wore a black dress with a boutonniere. Today's flower was a pink rose. "Good afternoon, ladies. Did you already read through all those books you bought recently?"

Betty laughed. "Oh, no, Miss Baldwin! We are here on a special mission today."

Miss Baldwin's narrow eyebrows arched. "Really? How can I be of service?"

Betty lowered her voice. "Can we get away from others?"

Miss Baldwin's eyes widened. This was not a common request. She stepped aside and pointed to a secluded reading area. "Is this sufficient?"

The sisters smiled and walked towards two rather worn leather couches. There was a table in front of the couches for readers to leave their books when finished. The spot was cordoned off from the rest of the shop by the imposing bookshelves. Once the three got seated, Miss Baldwin looked at them expectantly.

Betty took a deep breath and began. "We found a very old document inside a novel that had been donated to a white elephant sale. We have turned it over to the police."

"Because we think it is really very valuable," Kate interjected.

"And we want to know where to go to evaluate its worth," added Betty.

"My, my!" Miss Baldwin responded. "This is not a normal question for a bookshop! But I think I have some suggestions. Before anything else, you should get it authenticated, however. And for that I would go to the Massachusetts Historical Society. Absolutely the first step!" She stood up, indicating that was all for now. The sisters looked at each other and nodded. They had assumed rightly. They stood up.

"Thank you for your information, Miss Baldwin. We will head down to Boylston Street and talk to someone this afternoon." Betty picked up her purse.

"This is fascinating. May I ask the nature of this document?" Miss Baldwin asked with a not so professional curiosity.

"We think it is a list of some kind. Quite old. 1600s." Kate responded.

Miss Baldwin's face dropped. A list is not quite so exciting. "Well, good luck this afternoon, ladies. Keep me informed about the review of your document," she added as she walked away to help another customer. The sisters walked towards the exit.

"That was quick thinking, Kate," Betty said in an under-tone. "Miss Baldwin seemed a little too excited. She would, probably, tell everyone she knew, if you had given her the whole story." Betty opened the door to the street and walked out.

Kate nodded. "That was my thought, exactly. She is a bit high-strung." The wind had picked up as the two walked across the street and got into the roadster. "Brrr. If it gets much cooler, I will have to get out my fall coat!" Betty laughed at her complaining sister as she got into the roadster and started the engine.

"You should know that a light jacket, alone, won't do it when the leaves start falling!" she teased as she pulled into traffic and headed for Tremont St. It was only 5 minutes in light traffic to get to the Society's imposing Colonial Revival building. Looking to park, she realized that the curbside parking was full for two blocks.

"I guess you will warm up with a little stroll," Betty smirked as they got out of the car. They quickly walked the two short blocks and mounted the steps to the double glass doors.

At the front information desk, the receptionist was a seated middle-aged man with a pince-nez at the end of his nose. He looked over the top to greet them.

"Good afternoon, ladies. How can I be of service?"

Betty took the lead. "We are looking for someone to guide us in evaluating an old document."

"How old are you thinking it is?" he asked.

"Probably from the 1600s," Betty replied.

"Are you sure that you have something that old? Most of the historical items from around here have been classified for years and are in safe keeping." His tone was condescending, Kate thought.

"I am sure that the paper is quite brittle and the date "Anno Domini 1638" is written on it." Betty sniffed as she gave him the information.

"May I see it?" The man held out his hand.

"I do not have it with me. It is in police custody."

He stood up and made an inarticulate noise half way between a sniff and a grunt. "I believe you wish to speak to Mr. Benjamin. Please sit down over there and I will find out if he can see you now."

Within ten minutes, Mr. Benjamin, one of the curators, had the ladies in his office and seated across from his desk. They explained the whole story and asked for his opinion.

He leaned back in his brown leather upholstered chair and closed his eyes for 30 seconds. His fingertips met across his ample front and he made no move. Then he sat forward, putting his hands palm down on his desk. He looked intently at the two, eyes glistening.

"If this is as you say, then, this could be the find of the decade, even the century. I want to make an appointment with this Detective Roach and see this item for myself." The excitement in his voice was unmistakable.

Betty and Kate sat back in their chairs, relieved that he believed them. "As we said, it is in the custody of the police currently and it may take a few days before we can get the document, and the detective, over here," Kate added.

"My dear ladies, this is such a unique experience that I will interrupt myself from whatever I am doing to see you. Whenever you can come, I will be at your service." He stood up and walked around the desk. The sisters stood to leave. "Remember, we are available from 8am to 5pm, Monday through Friday."

After shaking hands, the two ladies left, excited to think they might have something solid to tell Casey.

After dinner, the sisters retired to their rooms to read. Kate had just begun "How Green Was Your Valley". She typically read for half an hour before Casey called to chat about their day.

It was 9:15 before Casey called. He had been working on a number of different reports and he was not a very fast typist.

After listening to his day, Kate had her own news. She sat up on the chaise and announced, "Mr. Benjamin from the Massachusetts Historical Society wants to meet you." "Why?" Casey asked cautiously.

"Betty and I went to talk to him today. He would love to see that document. But I told him it is in your custody, so you have to go with it."

Kate could hear Casey drumming his fingers on the table as he sat silently for 30 seconds. He took a breath. She smiled, knowing what he would say next.

"Ok. You have me there. When and where?"

"He said he will interrupt whatever he is doing to see the document. So, any time you are free."

She heard the flipping of pages as he went through his notebook. "How about Thursday morning? I have no appointments until afternoon."

"Not a thing earlier?"

"Ok, if it is only going to take an hour or so, I have 2 til 3:30 available tomorrow afternoon. How about I meet you in front of the Society at 2:15?"

Kate squealed with delight to have the time so soon. "I am sure that Betty will want to come, too," she advised him. "After all, she did most of the talking today."

"I am glad she got a few words in," Casey replied. "You do tend to take much of the conversation." And he laughed. "I am just teasing you, Kate, you know." Kate felt warm all over hearing his soothing baritone.

"I know. Say, before we hang up.... Is Joe there? I bet Betty would like to hear a word from him."

"Sure. I will get him. Good night, my cute little brunette!"

TUESDAY AFTERNOON

Mr. Benjamin was sitting at his desk, with his desk lamp shining on the item of focus. He had a watchmaker's loupe on over his glasses and white cotton gloves on. Casey, Betty and Kate were watching him intently from their seats. Not a word had been spoken in ten minutes as he examined the document and took notes. Finally, he took off the loupe and put the document into a large manila envelope marked 'Police Evidence'. Then he took off his gloves and pushed his chair away from the desk. Looking up at the three, Benjamin walked around to the front of the desk to get closer.

"I think you have something, here," he pronounced. "The print is quite faded, yes, but with a magnifying glass, you can read it."

"So, sir, what is it, exactly?" Casey asked, notebook in ready.

"This is a list of items that Nathaniel Eaton had requested for the Newtown school before he would agree to be the headmaster."

"Who is Nathaniel Eaton? And what is the Newtown school?" Kate was puzzled.

"Nathaniel Eaton was the first headmaster of the college

that was eventually named after John Harvard. The school was in one building with nine or twelve boys and Eaton's family."

"I never knew that!" The three looked at each other.

"What kind of items are on the list?" asked Casey, the most practical of the three.

"Bags of apple seeds or seedlings, a printing press, two female servants, one male servant, not counting the agricultural workers," Benjamin read off.

Casey wrote down what the curator had read. "This is interesting," he said looking up. "So, I assume that this document has value?"

"It certainly has. I would need to consult with others over an approximate value. But it is upward of four digits, I can assure you." Betty and Kate's eyes opened wide. Mr. Benjamin grinned. "Yes, indeed, ladies." Looking at Casey's puzzled face, he added. "I will speak with Freeman Appraisal Service, of course, but I can probably estimate their quote."

The curator took a deep breath and stood up a little straighter. His grin disappeared and he became all business. He walked back to his seat. He sidled into his chair, twisting to get comfortable. Putting his hands on the desk, he looked judgmental. "Now, tell me, again. Where did you get this document from?" He sighed, in a ragged, uncontrolled way, looking at each of the three. His eyes were half shut as he looked accusingly at them.

"We told you yesterday," Betty said, a bit defensively, aware that the tone had changed.

"I am to believe that a 17th century document dropped out of a book printed 25 years ago." Mr. Benjamin's eyelids drooped as he looked at them. He was suspicious.

"Sir, I am with the Boston police and the book was handed to me, still wrapped in the tissue paper from the white elephant sale." Casey glared at the curator.

"In that case, sir," the older man returned. "You have a larger problem on your hands than finding the value of a document. This," he said, pointing to the envelop. "This is a part of American history and has been somewhere and probably has been stolen from someone." His voice raised as he finished the sentence.

"I am sure we all have had that in the back of our heads, sir," Casey retorted. "It was not my idea to bring this to you, but the girls," he cocked his head towards them. "Well, they tend to take the bull by its horns."

Benjamin looked at the two sisters and sighed. Then he turned back to Casey. "Detective, I can appreciate that the document is evidence, yet, I am requesting that you leave it in my expert hands. I would like to show it to several select people in the next few days and get a good estimate.

Plus, I want to discuss with them the possibility of it being known to anyone. A document does not exist for 300 years without someone having heard about it."

Casey sat back to think for a moment. His boss would not like to hear that he made a deal with a museum curator for some evidence of a crime. "No. I am sorry. That destroys the trail of possession of the evidence. But, what I can do is have a patrolman accompany the document and be available whenever you need to show it. Within reason, of course."

"Of course," Benjamin reiterated. He picked up the envelop and handed it to Casey. "Let no one touch the document without clean white gloves," he admonished before getting up to walk the three to the door.

"Thank you for letting me be the first to see this," the curator turned on the charm, again, as they shook hands and left.

Betty walked out with her nose in the air. Kate saw and said nothing. Casey laughed. "Don't get too upset, Betty. He is only seeing from his own perspective. This kind of stuff does not just show up." The three walked out the doors of the Society and down the stairs. "Thank you for setting up this appointment, Kate. I have to get back to the precinct." He winked. "Talk to you tonight." Casey headed for his four-year old green Opel sedan and the sisters headed for their Mercedes Benz.

"I am insulted!" Betty whined as soon as the two were alone. "Benjamin dressed us down as if we were fools."

"Casey came as a favor to us. But it is a good thing that he did! He really has more important things on his agenda than books and papers." Kate slipped into the passenger seat and fixed her hat. "I think we can do something to further this investigation."

Betty looked over to her and pointed the car key at her. "You are not going to get us into trouble, are you?"

"No. This is well within bounds!" she smiled. "Let's go see Miss Baldwin, again. I have an idea."

Betty drove the roadster back over to West St. and found a parking spot only a block away. Checking her lipstick in the rear-view mirror, she got out, checked her purse for paper and pen and followed Kate across the street.

Irene Baldwin, sporting a white rose, was at the front checkout desk when she saw them come in. "My, my! Our little bookstore is becoming a very popular place for you two! How can I help you today?" She took a step down from the raised dais where the desk stood and walked over to them, smiling a welcome.

"We may need a little help in tracing a book, Miss Baldwin," Kate began.

"You do have different questions, Miss Hadley! Let's go

into our little lounge area and we can talk." She directed them into the same cordoned off area where they had sat the day before.

Betty sat and pulled out her pen and notepad. Kate sat next to her on the couch. Miss Baldwin sat expectantly. "We told you about the questionable document." The saleslady nodded. "Well, we found it in a used book. We are trying to find out who bought that book and where."

The older woman pursed her lips with distain. But she kept her welcoming smile in her eyes and took a deep breath. "Tell me the name of the book. Do you have it with you?"

"No. It is in police custody as evidence," Kate answered.

"Evidence? Of a crime?" Miss Baldwin physically seemed to shrink into the leather chair.

"Yes, it appears that someone wanted something in the shopping bag a lady was carrying. That is the only thing that seemed the least bit valuable in there," Betty explained.

"So, the police decided to keep it for now," Kate added. "Anyhow, it is Charles Dickens' A Christmas Story. About 25 years old, judging from the copyright date." She described the cover and the condition. "Considering its age, I assume if it was sold, it would have been sold on consignment."

"Has a book like that been sold here in the past few months?" Betty questioned.

Miss Baldwin stood up. "We keep a very tight inventory, my own design." She smiled proudly. "We have every book entered into our system and we record when it was bought and when it was sold. Let me take you into my file room and find out." She led the way out of the seating area, past the rows of wooden bookshelves to the back of the store. She pushed open a door marked "Private" and held the door open for the sisters. The room was small and was filled with card catalog sized file cabinets and an old oak table with four chairs.

"Just have a seat, dears. I shan't be more than a minute," she assured them. The sisters took off their jackets and made themselves comfortable while the saleslady turned to the file drawers and began her search. "We keep this log because when people sell their books on consignment. We need to be able to trace each book," she explained without turning around to them. "The books are filed under the title. There would not be too many of that title." She paused as she looked through the descriptions of the three books with that title. "Ah! Here we are!" she added whirling around on a heel and holding up the index card.

She stepped over to the table and proudly placed the card in front of the ladies.

Betty and Kate looked down at it and read the neat type-written words. Kate pointed to the bottom and glanced at

Betty. "It hasn't been sold?"

Miss Baldwin's face fell and she snatched up the card. "It... it was misfiled? How... how could that be?" The bottom of the card read "sold to..." and the rest was blank. She held the card to her chest and a look of desperation came over her. "My filing system failed!"

"Who does the filing?" Betty pulled out her notepad and pen to quickly make a diagram to help her thoughts.

"We all do. Every night, we type up all sales for the day and file. Each does her own sales, whether it is a new book or a used." Poor Miss Baldwin sat down hard on a chair, looking wilted. "What did I do wrong?"

"I do not think you did anything wrong, Miss Baldwin," Kate responded quickly. "But I think someone here did." She took the card from Miss Baldwin's shaking hand and read it. "This says that the book arrived, as a used book, only two weeks ago. So, I think that anyone who has not worked here in the past two weeks, or since Saturday, is not to blame." She looked intensely at Betty. "We had better talk to all the salespeople here," nodding to indicate to Betty to agree.

Betty picked up on the hint right away. "Oh, indeed. The sooner the better. You never know who might remember something." She glanced at the older woman to watch her reaction. Miss Baldwin sat up in her chair and looked at the sisters.

"You can do that today?" She looked at her watch, which read after 4:00 and, then, from one to the other.

Betty glanced up at her sister, who nodded her head half an inch, then looked back to the saleslady. "I am sure we can start," she responded. Holding up her notebook, she added, "I am prepared."

Miss Baldwin took a deep breath, stood and smoothed her dress. "I will tell Iris to come back. It takes her a while to do her closing, so she can be first. She can take care of closing out her register when she is done." She smiled grimly and walked out, leaving the sisters alone.

Iris was a big-boned blonde, about 30, with a cheap Sears outfit in black and a suspicious expression on her face. She stood at the entry to the room, arms crossed. "You need to see me?"

Betty looked up from what she was writing in her notepad. "Oh, you must be Iris. Come on in. We are trying to track a book for Miss Baldwin. Have a seat."

Iris cautiously walked in and took a seat at the other end of the table. She put her folded hands on the table. "What book?"

"Charles Dickens' A Christmas Carol. An old copy, probably 25 years old or so. Blue cover, with gold on the front." Kate felt uncomfortable around this woman. She had shifty eyes.

"I don't recognize that."

"That is strange. It was only two weeks ago that it came into the store. You do not do much consignment work."

"Oh, yes. I remember, now. It was an old book. I put it in the shelf."

"Did you see it after that?"

"No. I do not like Christmas stories." Her eyes looked back and forth between the sisters. "Do you own this place?"

"No, we are just helping a friend. Thank you for coming back here. You can return to your work." Betty told her.

"Good." Iris's pug nose was up in the air. She scraped the floor with the chair and left without a word.

"Friendly sort, isn't she?" Kate said under her breath. Betty smirked, then quickly reset her mouth as the next lady came in.

"Hi, I am Linda. Miss Baldwin said you wanted to speak to me?" A bubbly 20-year old, Linda had a dress that was obviously too large and ten years out of date. Her strawberry blonde hair clashed with the dull grey and blue stripe, but she acted as if she didn't notice. She took a seat before they invited her to.

"Thank you for interrupting your schedule, Linda, "Betty

began. "Have you seen, in the past few weeks, a copy of 'A Christmas Carol?' Old. Blue cover. It was brought in on consignment."

Linda's smiling face was plastered on as she looked down at her hands. They were not sure she heard the question. But after 30 seconds, her head popped up. "I never knew we HAD a copy!" She tilted her head. "What happened to it?"

"It is gone and had only been in the store two weeks."

"Well, I didn't sell it." Linda pronounced. "You should ask Jackie. She remembers most everything." She stood up. "Sorry I couldn't help." Then she turned around and walked out.

The sisters looked at each other aghast. "I-I think she is rude!" Kate stuttered. Betty followed the girl's back as she walked away.

A few minutes later, a tall, lanky brunette, in a pin-striped suit walked up to the doorjamb and knocked. "May I come in?" she asked softly. Betty welcomed her in and invited her to sit.

"I am Jackie. Miss Baldwin said you wanted to see me?"

"Thank you for coming in, Jackie. We are looking for a book," Betty began.

Jackie frowned at them. "We have plenty in the front." She pointed out the door. Kate raised an eyebrow.

"This is a particular book, 'A Christmas Carol', by Dickens. It's an old book, blue cover. It came in two weeks ago."

Jackie frowned again. "That one." She stared into space for a moment. "Last week, I saw Iris with a customer in those shelves. They had it out. Whether he bought it or not, I could not tell you. I was busy."

"What made you remember that?" Kate asked.

"Well, you have met Iris. She is so big. And the fellow was so short. Mutt and Jeff, you know." She tittered.

Kate's eyes widened, remembering what Mrs. Stevens had said. "Did you notice his eyes?" she asked.

"No. They were too far away and the lighting between racks is not like outdoors. I think he was blonde, if that helps" Jackie shook her head.

"Would you possibly recognize him again if you saw him?" Betty asked.

"Well, maybe if he was standing next to Iris. I only saw him that once." Jackie looked at the two. "Is that all?"

The sisters thanked her and Jackie left. Looking at each other, the two pairs of eyes danced with excitement.

"He sounds a little like the man Mrs. Stevens described," Kate whispered excitedly.

Betty stuffed her notebook and pen into her purse and pulled the car keys out. "Let's go home. It's getting close to dinner time, anyhow." Looking at her watch. "5:10. It is past time for this store to close, anyhow."

Miss Baldwin caught them walking up the main aisle towards the front door. Her corsage looked a little wilted. "Did you find out anything useful?"

"We may have," Betty responded, hesitantly. "We have some ideas, so we will go home and talk about it tonight. If we have any more questions, I am sure we will be calling you in the morning." Betty gave her a big smile and rushed out the door.

WEDNESDAY MORNING

Betty and Kate were on their second cups of coffee and reading the morning newspaper at the breakfast table. Betty always started with the society page; Kate, with the editorial page.

Suddenly, Betty began to cough and dropped her cup on the table. The paper fell from her hand to the floor. She was bent over, hitting herself in the chest. Alarmed, Kate jumped up and ran around to the other side of the table. She slammed her hand up against Betty's back, making Betty arch backwards.

"Why did you hit so hard?" Betty sputtered once she could stop coughing.

"I thought you were dying!"

"No, I just saw that article! And swallowed wrong!"

"What article?" Kate asked as she grabbed the paper from where it had landed. Betty pointed to the bottom of the last page.

"Antique shop robbed," Kate read. "Hmm. Sounds interesting." She took the section back to her chair and read out loud. "Percy Stanley, proprietor of Ye Olde Junk Shoppe, Center St. in Jamaica Plain, reports that early last week, his shop was broken into and several items stolen. Among the items taken were an early 19th century music box worth $100 and an old document mentioning Harvard, which has no known value. The book shop was recently opened and had no hours posted, yet. Mr. Stanley was still bringing in inventory. He has no knowledge of the perpetrator and the public is asked to be on the lookout for these items." She put the paper down and looked at her sister. "A week later, and it finally gets into the newspaper!" She scowled at Betty, watching her wipe coffee from her blouse. "Coffee down the wrong way, huh?" Betty nodded. "I am not surprised, after reading this." Kate looked at the mantle clock. "Casey has been at work for an hour. I think we should talk to him and tell him of this. I'll bet he has not seen this article."

Betty cleared her throat. "I think we should discuss the next step with Miss Baldwin's girls, first." She went to the buffet and opened a drawer, taking out pen and paper. "Let's see what we have, now."

They proceeded to review everything they had found out, including the new piece of information, including the theft.

"Maybe, before calling Casey, Kate, we should call this fellow and find out if the document is the same one," Betty concluded.

Kate's eyes brightened. "His business is not going to be in the directory, since it is new. We will have to go to Jamaica Plain and try our luck."

"I will bet this article will bring him some business. He probably has finished bringing his inventory to the store."

"Oh, that is most likely true," Kate nodded in agreement.

Her nose wrinkled as she watched Betty try to get the coffee out without success. "You will have to change that blouse, first. How long until you are ready?"

"Give me half an hour. You call for the car and tell Cook we won't be here for lunch." Betty ignored the rest of her coffee and left to change.

At 10:00, the sisters were in the Mercedes-Benz roadster headed towards Center St. in Jamaica Plains. The traffic on Brighton Ave. was busy, so it was almost 10:30 before Betty pulled up to a small shop in a somewhat run-down area of Jamaica Square.

Kate squinted at the window. "It looks open. I can't tell with those dirty windows. Let me get out." She got out of the car and walked to the window. A temporary sign said "Ye Olde Junk Shoppe". She saw a man moving around and motioned to Betty to get out.

Cringing as she touched the dirty doorknob with her white gloves, Kate turned it and the two walked in. Some of the inventory had not been put up, judging from the number of boxes sitting on the floor. The man turned at the bell and broke into a smile. He was a middle-aged man who obviously had gained weight since the last time he bought a pair of pants. He seemed a friendly sort.

The girls introduced themselves as friends helping out a lady from church. "We saw the article in today's Herald about your break-in last week," Betty said, getting out her pen and notebook. "And we have a few questions about the document you say is missing."

"Yes, yes," Mr. Stanley welcomed the opportunity to speak. He pulled up a few old dusty chairs as he spoke.

"The police took an inventory of missing items. There were six missing. I do not know what else to tell you."

"Mr. Stanley, we are not, strictly speaking, with the police. So, could you tell us about the document again?" Betty asked. The sisters sat down gingerly after wiping the seats with their gloves.

He eyed them suspiciously and then shrugged. "There is little to say. I bought a few boxes of used items from a man cleaning out a tenement around about here. They were just old nuisances and had been in the attic for years when he bought the house last year. He just wanted them out. So, I bought the lot for $20. The document was in a big manila envelope, in the box."

"Did you read the document?"

"If I read every document or book I brought into this store, I would get nothing done. It was really old and yellowy. I figured I would get to it, eventually, when I finished cataloguing everything." The sisters' faces fell.

He crossed his legs and lit a cigarette. "I can't tell you much. But it did have a date on it. It was really faded. 1638, I think."

Kate's eyes opened wide. Betty's mouth gaped. "1638?"

"That's what I think I read." He blew out smoke, put the cigarette aside and leaned forward. "Why is that interesting?"

"Our friend found a book, on Saturday, with an old document in it. The document was dated 1638," Kate replied.

His eyebrows went up. "That is one damned interesting coincidence!"

"Or, is it?" Betty replied. "I think, with the timing, it is not just a coincidence. Would you recognize it again, if you saw it?"

"Oh, probably. It had a rip on the upper left-hand corner, cutting off the first letter of the first sentence." Betty and Kate looked at each other, eyes wide open, but said nothing. "It was faded and I didn't have time to read it all. To me, it was just an old grocery list, or something. But I didn't take the time, like I said before. I was moving in."

"Had you figured on a price for it?"

"No. Probably $5. It was really old!" He tried to apologize for the high price.

Kate was already opening her purse. She pulled out a $10 bill and showed it to him. "Mr. Stanley, I would like to purchase that document."

"I don't have it. I told you," he said adamantly.

"Yes. But, you see, I think we have it. Or, rather, the police have it. They just don't know yet that your document is our document."

His furrowed brow showed his confusion. "My document

is with the police?" He paused for a moment and debated. "All right!" He held out his hand.

Kate pulled the bill back a little. "I want a receipt, first," she said, smiling encouragingly. The bill dangled between her thumb and forefinger.

Stanley got up, went to the cash register and grabbed a receipt pad. He wrote up the bill of sale and handed it to her, plucking the bill out from her fingers.

Kate smiled up at him. "Thank you, Mr. Stanley!" She handed the receipt to Betty, who placed it in her notebook.

Betty stood up and tucked the notebook away. "By the way, can we also get the name of the fellow you bought the boxes from? And his address or phone number?" Stanley shrugged his shoulders.

"Why not?" He grabbed a piece of notepaper and wrote the information on it. Betty smiled at him when she received it. "Thank you, Mr. Stanley," she said graciously as the two waltzed out the door.

Back in the car, the ladies were overwhelmed with their success. "I think Casey will thank us for all this work. We are making his job very easy." Kate beamed.

"So, do you think we should be telling him, yet?" Betty cautioned.

"What do you have in mind?"

"Let's try to contact that fellow who sold Mr. Stanley the

boxes. A Mr. Peterson. His address is on Paul Gore Street." Betty looked up trying to picture a map of the area. "That is not too far from here. Let's run over and see if he is home."

"I would be interested in meeting a fellow who throws away such important documents. Wonder if he has more," Kate pondered.

It was only a five-minute drive to 253 Paul Gore Street, a typical triple-decker Boston mainstay. Betty and Kate were looking at each other, debating about which door to knock on, when a young man came out the left front door. He lit a cigarette and saw the car. Coming down the steps to their car, it was obvious that his clothes were spattered with paint. He was, apparently, taking a work break.

"Can I help you ladies?" The pleasant-faced fellow bent over to the window. He smiled as Kate rolled down the window.

"We are looking for a Mr. Peterson," Kate smiled back.

"Junior or senior?" he quipped. Kate sat, stunned, and was not sure how to answer. The young man, grinned. "I'm Keith Peterson, senior." Kate leaned towards the window a little. She liked this man's humor.

"Hi! I am Kate Hadley," she put out a hand. He took it and shook it.

Betty introduced herself and reached out across Kate to shake his hand, too.

"What can I help you with?"

"You sold some boxes of junk to Mr. Stanley a few weeks ago. He was opening a junk shop. Do you remember?"

"Sure, I do. He had put an ad in one of the papers, looking for stuff. I bought this place less than a year ago. Gradually fixing it up. I found bunches of boxes all over and didn't want to go through them. So, I gave some to him." He grinned. "$20 for a few boxes. Not bad."

"Do you know where any of the stuff came from?" Kate asked.

Peterson looked at her quizzically. "I don't know. It was all here when I bought the house. Why?"

"Someone stole some of the items out of the shop. We were wondering why," Betty answered.

"Which items?" Patterson asked.

"The one we are interested in is a very old document on yellowed paper."

"Oh. That one. I found it in the attic, in a box with a bunch of stuff. It was in a large envelope. I was going to throw it away. It looked like an old grocery list. But it had the year 1638 on it. I figured someone could determine what it really was. Not me. I don't do history or anything like that."

"Who sold you this house, if you don't mind my asking," Betty interrupted when an idea popped into her head. She nudged Kate and winked when her sister turned around.

"Oh, that would be old Mr. Knapp." The sisters' ears pricked up at the name. "He had this house for fifty years or so. He is in a nursing home, now." Mr. Peterson sat down on the grass beside the car. He was still tall enough to see over the window sill of the door. "He liked to hold on to stuff. I don't."

"Do you know which nursing home?" Kate hadn't recognized the surname as being from the document when he mentioned it. But, her mind was already planning ahead.

"It's St. Elizabeth's on Sheridan. I moved him there, myself, which is the only reason I know." His eyes squinted into the car. "Why are two classy ladies, like yourselves, wandering around Jamaica Plain talking to young men about junk?"

Kate laughed out loud at the question. "We can't help ourselves when something pricks our interest. We have to hunt it down as far as we can."

Mr. Patterson smiled and said, "Oh, I see." Then he got up off the grass and wiped his backside. "Well, I wish you ladies luck in whatever you do. Sounds like fun, if you like that kind of stuff." Betty started the engine and he backed away from the curb, shaking his head.

Kate started to roll up the window and caught a few words, "all over a silly piece of paper." The sisters looked at each other and laughed it off.

Pulling away from the curb, Betty drove over to Sheridan St. "I know you are excited, but I am hungry and I think we should stop for lunch, before we try to meet Mr. Knapp. What do you think?"

"I am ready to eat, Betty. It's past noon."

"How about a little delicatessen near here? There has to be one at Egleston Square." Betty drove around the block and headed towards the commercial area. Soon enough they spotted Suffolk Delicatessen on one of the streets, parked and went in.

Sitting at one of the booths, waiting for their order of Reuben sandwiches, Betty pulled out her notes and they reviewed them.

"So, we have an elderly man who collects things. Mr. Knapp. He sells a house full of junk to Mr. Patterson, who doesn't like junk." Kate laughed. "Patterson sells some of the junk to a junk dealer, Mr. Stanley, who loves junk, but doesn't take the time to review the stuff he bought, because he bought boxes of it all at once."

"In order for someone to take the items, and not ransack the store, that someone had to have an idea of what he was looking for," Kate pointed out.

Betty looked at her, thoughtfully. "You have a point, dear sister." She looked at her notes, again, and back at Kate. "Someone knew what he was looking for."

"Or stumbled over a prize document within minutes of getting there." Kate screwed up her face, trying to make sense of this. "Who breaks into an unorganized junk shop?"

"That does not make sense, does it?" Betty tilted her head, looking into the distance. It took at least ten seconds before she looked back at Kate. "How much do you want to bet that whoever broke into the junk shop knew Mr. Knapp before then?"

"Why would you say so...OH! He took just a few things that were not yet displayed, so he knew what he was looking for. So, he must have known where they were from!" Kate virtually bounced in her seat, eyes glistening. She pointed her finger at Betty, excitedly pronouncing Betty's thoughts.

The blonde waitress, whose nametag said "Winnie", returned with the two plates, watching the two intensely chatter. When they didn't notice, she cleared her throat loudly. They looked up at her and realized what she was holding. They laughed and moved their cups and purses apart sufficiently for the waitress to place the platters down.

"You are having a very interesting conversation, I see. Please, do not let me interrupt." Winnie began to step away when Betty called her back.

"I know this is a long shot, but do you know an old man named Mr. Knapp? He lived a few blocks from here."

"Sure, old man Knapp. He came every Sunday morning for breakfast. For years. He had a triple decker that he talked about like it was his prize possession."

Both sisters stared at the waitress. "You actually talked to him?" Kate queried, shocked that Betty's question could be answered.

"Sure. Do you know he is the great-great-something grandson of a president of Harvard? You would never know looking at him or that junk-filled house. He's just a little old man," the waitress added. "But cute," Winnie winked. She looked at the empty cups. "Here, let me get the coffee pot. You are out." She waltzed away to grab a pot.

"Who would think?" Betty turned in awe to Kate. The waitress returned with the pot and poured their cups full before they even tasted their lunches.

"We are going to try to visit him after lunch," Betty told Winnie, trying to get more information out of the woman.

"Yea, that's too bad about his moving to the old folks' home, but he shouldn't be alone, either."

"Do you know who took over his place?" Kate asked, looking up at Winnie under half closed lids.

"I heard it was a young couple. But that's all. I wouldn't know them if they walked up to me." She shrugged her shoulders. "Tell Mr. Knapp that Winnie and the girls from Suffolk say hi, will you?"

"I will make sure to. Thanks, Winnie!" Betty returned. They left a generous tip when they left.

On the way to St. Elizabeth's on Sheridan, Kate was pondering on something Winnie had said about Knapp's junk-filled house. "I wonder how she knew." Kate pointed out as they drove along the residential streets.

"Either she had been in his house or she knew someone

who had and that someone had talked about it." Betty responded.

After they pulled up to the large old building, the sisters

checked their lipstick in the rear-view mirror and fixed their hats before getting out of the car. It was a bright day, warm for mid-October, and the glare off all the windows made them cover their eyes. Looking up at the windows of the institution, they spotted many white heads looking down at them. Kate waved and several waved back. Kate smiled at them, then turned to Betty. "Don't ever suggest putting Dad in a place like this," she murmured as they walked in the big front door.

At the reception desk was a heavy-set woman, dressed all in white, reading a book. As they approached, she looked up. "May I help you?" she said, eyes darting back and forth from her book to the sisters.

"Is there a Mr. Knapp living here?"

"Let me look," she responded, turning from the book to a tickler file on the desk. She looked through the cards and pulled one out. "Here you are. Room 240. Second floor." She pointed to the stairs at the back of the reception room, then looked back to her book.

The two, high heels clicking on the polished wood floors, walked upstairs. They found room 240 and knocked. Within a minute, a wizened old man, not much taller than Betty's 5'2, opened the door halfway.

"You already gave me lunch..." he started. Then started.

"You aren't one of the nurses!"

Betty grinned. "Mr. Knapp, I am Elizabeth Hadley and this is my sister, Katherine. We were in the neighborhood and had some questions to ask. Do you have a few minutes?"

"I got nothing but time, now," was the response as he opened the door further. "Come on in!" The room was sparsely furnished with an iron bed, a dresser, and one black, worn Barcalounger. Two wooden chairs and a table were under the window. There was a radio in the corner, next to the big chair. Kate cringed to see the little he was obligated to live with.

"You ladies can have the chairs. If you don't mind, I like my big soft chair." He hobbled over to his comfortable chair. "I know what you are thinking. Why would a man move to a place like this? I just didn't want to do for myself, anymore." He eased himself onto the chair and pushed it back into recliner mode, folded his hands together over his shallow middle and turned to the two. "So, why are you here to talk to me?"

"Mr. Knapp, we found a paper in a book. It looks like this paper was stolen from the junk shop where Mr. Patterson had sold some boxes of your old stuff."

"I told him to look through that stuff before he got rid of it!" he barked. "Young people don't listen!"

Betty held up her hand. "Please, sir! He looked at everything but did not realize what he had. He thought he would give it to someone who could identify it."

"Yeah, and...?"

"The shop was broken into and that paper was taken before the proprietor could study it?"

"Why the hell didn't the proprietor take care of it earlier?"

Kate joined in. "He was just opening. He hadn't sorted out everything yet."

The old man rocked the chair a bit, contemplating. "So how did you get it?"

"It appeared in a book at a white elephant sale. We are trying to figure out how," Kate replied.

"That is why we came to speak with you," Betty interjected, pulling her notebook out. "We have some idea that whoever stole it, may have known you."

Knapp raised an eyebrow. "I don't know no thieves."

"We think you might know a handyman who decided to become a thief, or something like that," Betty responded.

"Specifically, a very short man with funny yellow-ish eyes." Kate leaned forward to watch his expression.

Knapp closed his eyes and leaned his head against the back of the recliner. His lips puckered and moved in and out a little. It took 30 seconds before he opened his eyes and sat up. "I remember a fellow like that. About a year ago. Just before I sold. He wanted to help me around the house. He didn't seem strong enough to carry all those boxes out. And I told him so. Then he wanted to go through the attic and help hisself to whatever was useful. I said no, it's all or nothing. So, he left. Just saw him the one time."

"Would you remember his name?"

"Nah. He didn't impress me. I don't think I asked."

"Would you recognize him again?" Kate probed.

"Probably. He had those funny eyes and he was short. Shorter than me, and that's saying some." He licked his lips and chortled.

"We are trying to find out if that paper is worth something." Betty stood and Kate followed suit. "Thank you for helping us. We will let you know what we find, if you would like."

"Well, sure. There was one or two things in those boxes that were family heirlooms, I was told. I never could figure out which ones."

"We are thinking of an old sheet of paper. Very faded, very yellowed."

"Ha!" the old man barked. "I thought it was a grocery list. Didn't have the heart to pitch it. Belonged to an ancestor, I heard tell. If I am still around when you figure it out, let me know. I'd be interested."

The girls shook hands with the old man and let themselves out. Back in the car, the two started to giggle.

"He is such a sweet old fellow," Betty pronounced.

"And he knows that fellow, whoever he is. At least by sight.

We have to talk to Casey about this," Kate concluded.

"Let's invite Casey and Joe over for a late dessert," Betty suggested. She looked at her watch. It was now 3:30. "If we get home by 4, perhaps we can talk Cook into making a fancy dessert." Kate agreed and sat back for the half hour drive through the streets of Boston to the house on Beacon Hill.

Casey Roach and Joe Talbot were detectives in different precincts of the BPD and roommates in a pleasant flat in South Boston. They were also dating the two socialite sisters who fancied themselves detectives. Casey blamed it on the new movies coming out. Kate had gotten more enamored of the idea after they had gone out to see the latest Thin Man movie, entitled appropriately, "Another Thin Man".

"What do you think the girls are up to, inviting us over for coffee and chocolate cake, in the middle of the week?" Joe asked Casey, who was at the wheel of his four-year old Opel.

"They are interested in that document I told you about. They are serious enough to have talked about it with the curator of the Massachusetts Historical Society. He was duly impressed. So, I am thinking they found something else about it," Casey concluded, pulling onto Beacon St.

"Ah, coffee and cake to announce they found a piece of the puzzle!" Joe proclaimed. "If they find too much evidence in their detecting, we are going to get fat!"

Casey laughed. "We will just have to work harder, Joe, and keep the fat off." A moment later, the green car pulled up in front of the Hadley home on Louisburg Square.

"Eight o'clock on the nose," Joe announced as he stepped

out of the car. Casey, 4" taller, had to duck to avoid hitting his head on the frame.

Kate and Betty opened the door and welcomed the men. Walking directly into the dining room, the men were pleased to see the cake already on the table.

"Are you going to tell us why you invited us here?" Joe asked Betty. "What's with the cake?" Betty smiled up at him.

"You must wait. We have some news!"

Joe smiled, shook his head and sat down. Casey sat across from him. Betty sat next to Joe with the transcription of her notes. As Betty read the notes, Kate cut the cake and passed the plates around. The men were impressed with the report, as well as the cake.

"You did this all today?" Casey asked, with a piece of chocolate cake hanging on his fork.

The sisters nodded.

"I am impressed," Joe added after swallowing his bite. He smiled approvingly at Betty and Betty grinned back.

"So, let me get this straight." Casey started after putting down his coffee. "Mr. Knapp had a bunch of ancient junk. He leaves it to Patterson, who doesn't want it. Patterson sells it to the junk man for a relative pittance. Junk man has his place broken into and only a few conspicuous things are taken. And the short guy with the weird eyes is in the loop."

"That's what we said," the sisters said in duet. Kate laughed and turned to Casey.

"I thought you would be impressed!" She sat up straighter in her chair and raised her chin. "I think this young man is a thief and you should go after him."

Casey smirked and winked at Joe. "Yes, ma'am. Do you have a name, address or next of kin for me to start?" Joe half smiled at Casey's request.

Kate sagged. "No," she responded in a quiet voice. "I guess Betty and I had better keep looking for clues."

"Don't worry, honey," Betty assured her sister. "We are going to keep looking." She turned to Joe. "Do you have any ideas?"

"Well, if we can get a sketch of the guy, we could show it around...."

"We could go back to the bookstore and question Iris again. Maybe she remembers something about the little fellow that she did not mention."

Betty perked up. "As a matter of fact, she did seem a little uncomfortable with us."

Joe put down his coffee cup and turned to Betty. "Just remember that not all people who are uncomfortable with being questioned are guilty. Some people just do not like their lives interfered with. This Iris may be one of those."

Betty crossed her arms and looked at him askance. "You

did not see that woman. She is big and overbearing. I don't think she is the type to be shy about her life. I think she was not cooperating."

Joe raised his eyebrows. "You didn't mention that yesterday."

"I have been thinking about it all day as we have been questioning other people. She just did not sit right with me."

The phone rang in the hall. James picked it up and spoke momentarily. When he approached the dining room door with the phone, all four at the table turned around. "It is Joseph at Mrs. Stevens'. He sounds upset."

Betty, sitting closest to the door, put her hands out for the phone. "Good evening, Joseph," she began. The others watched her eyes open wider as she listened at the receiver. "Goodness! I happen to have the detective right here. Give us five minutes." She hung up and returned the phone to James. Turning back to the table guests, she pronounced, "We do not need to look for that short fellow's name and address. He has been caught at Mrs. Steven's."

Casey was the first to stand. "Let's go!" he directed, then flew out the door to grab his hat and coat from James. Joe followed. The girls flew up the stairs to grab their wraps from their rooms and were down the stairs and out the door by the time Casey had started the engine.

AT MRS. STEVENS'

Joseph opened the front door as soon as the four pulled up in the Opel. They rushed from the sidewalk, up the stairs to the stoop. Mrs. Stevens, in a dinner frock, stood behind the older butler, twisting her handkerchief. Betty and Kate both approached her, sympathizing with the older woman.

"Please, Mrs. Stevens, can we sit somewhere and chat?" Casey immediately took charge. The butler led them into a well-appointed parlor, done in dark green and soft pink. Betty sat beside the older woman on the couch. Casey and Kate sat on the loveseat and Joe took a chair separated from the couch by a small end table. After they all took seats, both Casey and Betty took out their notebooks. Casey, officially; Betty, due to curiosity.

"Where is the fellow right now?" Casey asked first.

"Joseph tied him up and left him with the gardener," Mrs. Stevens answered, teary-eyed.

"Why was the gardener here at 8:00 at night?" Casey leaned forward, looking intently at this whining woman.

"He had come to pick up some money to purchase mulch and other gardening items." Joseph replied for his boss.

"At night?" Casey was confused.

"It is that time of the year, sir. Much needs to be done in a short period. The gardener has so many customers and not enough time. It was just easier so that he could get a good start in the morning."

Casey shrugged his shoulders. His face wrinkled as he tried to process the needs of the rich.

"So, where is this thief and the gardener right now?" he asked, again.

Joseph again answered. "They are currently in the basement. Do you want to meet them?"

Casey looked puzzled. "Not yet, thank you, Joseph. I first want to picture what happened. Can you explain?"

Joseph took a step further into the parlor and glanced around the room. "It was about 8. The gardener, Mr. Savage, was explaining the list of items for which Mrs. Stevens was to pay. We heard sounds in the basement. The young man is not a competent thief if he makes that much noise." Casey raised an eyebrow and stifled a chuckle. But he did not interrupt. "The gardener had been in the basement, through an exterior accessway. He probably left it open because he was not yet finished."

"Why was the gardener in the basement?" Casey was chasing an idea.

"Mr. Savage keeps all the gardening tools down there. The garden is not big enough for a shed. He was checking to see if he had enough plant covers, mulch. The typical."

Casey nodded. "I see."

"When we heard the noise, Mr. Savage ran down the interior basement access stairs at the back of the house and we heard more noise. He called my name and asked me to bring down some rope. The thief is very small. Mr. Savage did not need my help with holding him down." The butler smirked. "He lassoed that young man pretty well."

Casey started at hearing the butler use the term 'lasso', but kept it to himself. He bowed his head to hide his smirk then looked up to thank Joseph for his help.

Joe looked at Casey and had seen his head bob. "I think we should go meet this little creep." He stood up and turned to the girls. "You stay up here with Mrs. Stevens. We will check it out." The men followed Joseph to the back of the house.

Betty's attention turned to Mrs. Stevens after she watched the men leave. She placed her hand on the other woman's arm, reassuringly. "Is there anything we can do for you, Mrs. Stevens?" she asked the older woman.

The poor woman had not said much, still in shock at the thought of someone breaking into her home. "I want him out of here," she whined. "How dare he!"

Joseph returned to the parlor. "The detective has requested I call for backup," he announced. Then he stepped into the foyer to call the precinct office.

Although the ladies heard voices, they did not hear what was said in the basement. Within ten minutes, there was a knock on the door and Joseph announced the police had arrived. They tipped their hats to the ladies as they passed by the door, following Joseph.

It did not take too long before the police were back up on the first floor, hauling a reluctant little man through the foyer. They stopped at the parlor door. "Did you want to take a look at this weasel before we haul him in?" Kate stood up, but Betty sat protectively next to Mrs. Stevens, who would not look.

Kate took two steps forward and examined the fellow. He was about the same height as her 5', the eyes were a pale hazel, tending towards yellow. His sandy hair, badly in need of a trim, was dirty and hanging in his eyes. He stared at her but didn't say a word. The two officers pulled him through the door and down to the car.

Casey walked up to Kate and put his arm around her shoulders. "He looks like the typical thief, doesn't he?" He chuckled. "Not too smart, from the two minutes of conversation I got out of him."

"What is his name?" Kate asked, moving a little closer.

"He says it's Paul Clancy. But, I won't know for sure until I look through the mugshots or verify some ID. He had nothing on him tonight."

"Did he say what he was looking for?"

"He wasn't saying much. We will talk to him tomorrow."

The mantle clock chimed 10. Casey turned to Joe. "Our time here is done. What say you?"

Joe agreed. "Work starts early in the morning. Are you ok,

Betty?" Betty had been quietly speaking with Mrs. Stevens. She patted the older woman's hand and stood up.

"I am ready," she announced. Turning back to the older lady, she asked, "Will you be fine tonight?"

"Oh, yes. Joseph and his wife Gwen are so good to me."

"You call if you need anything, alright?" Mrs. Stevens nodded in answer to Betty's question, but did not rise from her seat.

THURSDAY MORNING

"Here is a mention of last night's arrest, Kate!" Betty shook the section of paper that she was reading in order to fold it over. "I'll read it. It is short." She took a sip of her coffee and placed the cup back on the saucer before proceeding.

"'A break-in was reportedly stopped by the residents of a home on Beacon Hill last night. The owner of the home, Mrs. David Stevens, was not available for comment. Police arrived at 9:15 and picked up the perpetrator, who told police his name was Paul Clancy. Officers say he has been uncooperative and they cannot confirm his identity.'" She placed the paper down and looked at Kate. "Why does he not just cooperate and get away with a short prison term?"

"My first thought last night, when I saw that he was not talking, was that he is protecting someone," Kate returned, taking a thoughtful bite out of her strawberry-covered toast.

Betty sat back in her chair, mulling that idea. She lazily grabbed her coffee cup again, after Sally, the maid, had refilled it. "I think it is worth mentioning to the boys about this. It makes perfect sense, what you said, about him protecting someone."

"You know, Betty, I think that we should do it today, the first day they are trying to get him to tell them his story."

Betty glanced up at the mantle clock. "Almost 9. Dad won't

be home til 5:00 or so. We have the whole day in front of us. What do you say to a little ride down to the precinct?"

Kate took a last gulp of her coffee, pushed back her chair and stood up. "Give me half an hour and I will be ready." Leaving the breakfast room, she ran into James.

"Are you needing the car this morning, Miss?" he queried.

"Yes, please, James. In half an hour. Can it be ready?" She flashed an expectant smile.

"Ah, another case bubbling up, Miss!" James observed.

"Yes, indeed!" she said over her shoulder as she ran up the steps to the second floor.

At 9:55, Betty parked the Mercedes-Benz roadster along the curb, a half block from the precinct office. As the sisters checked their lipstick and hats, Joe Talbot came walking down the steps of the large building. Recognizing the roadster, he rushed over to greet the two as they got out.

"Hello, Betty!" he called out as he approached. "What are you doing here this morning?" he added as he got up close enough to pat her shoulder.

"Good morning, Joe," Betty welcomed him with a broad smile. "We read the morning Herald and came to a conclusion that Paul Clancy is hiding something and we wanted to talk it over with you and Casey."

"I was just in with him, as detectives assigned to the case, we were trying to hash out a few details. May as well go back in with you and listen to your line of reasoning" He offered his arm to Betty and turned to Kate. "Are you coming?" Kate beamed. She had not seen Betty so happy in a long time. She followed them in.

Being with a police detective, the sisters did not have to stop at the desk sergeant to register. Kate waved to the Sgt. Ryan, who waved back.

At Casey's open door, Joe knocked and stepped in, still arm in arm with Betty. "Look who I found!" he announced.

Casey looked up and stood immediately. "What brings you down, ladies?' He walked around the desk and leaned down to Kate to kiss her. "Sit down, please." The three took the wooden hard-backed chairs facing the desk and Casey sat on the edge of the desk, facing them.

"Betty and I saw this morning's Herald. We started discussing this Paul Clancy and why he might be unwilling to talk," Kate began, taking off her gloves. "We were thinking he might be protecting someone."

"So," Joe interjected. "You do not think he is a two-bit thief who saw something he wanted and tried to get it?"

"No," Betty answered emphatically. "I think he might be working for or with someone."

"We are going to go over to the bookstore and question Iris, one of the salesladies, this morning. Once we are done here." Kate reminded them. "She was seen helping Paul Clancy in the bookshelves," she added.

"I plan on going downstairs and talking to Clancy," Casey

explained. "Technically, our being there last night gives us the assignment. I will try using the protecting-someone-else idea a chance. Let's see how he responds."

"Here's a thought," Betty interrupted. She sat up straighter in her chair, hands on the arm rests. "That young man does not seem particularly intelligent. I could be wrong. But, if he is trying to steal a piece of parchment, how does he know it is worth a large amount of money. After all, he wouldn't chase after a $10 document with the risk of a year or two in jail. At the same time, I don't think he is crazy."

"Another argument for his working with or for someone else," Joe commented, patting Betty's hand in approval. She smiled up at him, tossing her blonde curls, a little, in response.

"Well, we seem to have our days planned out. Let's get together tonight or tomorrow night and see what we have," Casey suggested. He rolled his eyes at Joe. Despite the fact that this was an actual police case, at this point, he knew he was not going to get the girls to quit.

Back on the street, Joe and the sisters parted company. Getting back in the roadster, Betty and Kate headed the few blocks to Brattle Book Store.

Miss Baldwin was standing at her customary location near the front door, ready to greet customers. Her black dress had a yellow rose pinned to the left shoulder. Her nose wrinkled, as if she had just smelled something bad, when she saw the sisters walk through the door. It was only for a second, but Kate noted it. Miss Baldwin put on her greeting face and smiled.

"How can I help you ladies this morning?" she gushed.

"May we speak to Iris, again?" Kate asked. "We have one or two more questions."

The nose wrinkled again, momentarily. "If you would be so kind, please walk back to the office you were in the other day and I will send her back to you." She was abrupt but not rude and turned towards the checkout counter, where Iris was with a customer.

Kate and Betty got comfortable in the back office and were quietly discussing dresses for the upcoming holidays, when Iris walked in the open door.

"What do you want with me?"

"Please, Iris, have a seat," Kate insisted, pulling out the chair beside her own. Iris sat with her arms folded in front, quiet and surly.

"The other day when we spoke, you had a difficult time remembering a book that we asked you about." Betty stopped to regard Iris. There was no comment.

"Just before the store closed, we were speaking to Jackie and she remembered you with a man in the stacks where that book would have been placed. Do you remember that?"

"No."

"Do you know a short man named Paul Clancy?" Kate blurted.

Iris' eyes widened for a moment, then became slits. "No."

Kate noticed the eyes, a controlled reaction. Iris knew something. Kate nodded slightly to Betty to let her know something had happened.

"By the way, I didn't get your last name for my notes. What is it?" Betty asked to change the subject a little.

"Clausen."

Betty raised an eyebrow. She sat back in her chair and put her pen down. "Do you have any brothers or sisters?" she asked conversationally.

"I am one of twelve children." Iris was cautious.

"What are their names?" Kate understood where Betty was going.

"Steven, Pavel, Anders, Martin, Johan, Eliot, Britt, Wilhemine, Katrina, Margareta, Rebekka and Tina." She leaned forward in her chair, hands on her knees. "You did not invite me here to name my family. What do you want?"

Kate piped up. "Jackie saw you with a man who looks like the man who was arrested last night for breaking into a house. We were there. We saw him."

Iris glanced at Kate, sat back and crossed her arms, again. "I know nothing."

Betty's shoulders sagged. "All right. Thank you very much for coming back here. You can get back to work."

Iris pushed herself out of the old wooden armchair and left without a backward glance. Kate noticed that Iris' shoes were well scuffed.

Betty watched the big woman leave. "I think we have to approach this a different way. She will not help, for whatever reason." She shook her head. "Either she is not a cooperative sort, or she is somehow involved. But I have no clue how to determine which it is."

Kate moved her chair a little closer and leaned in to speak in a low voice. "Did you see her eyes when I asked her if she knew a short man named Paul Clancy?"

Betty thought a moment and responded equally low. "I saw your nod, so I knew something was noticed, but I wasn't watching her eyes. I was writing."

"She recognized that name. She is not the uncooperative type. She knows the name, or even the person. And she has a brother named Pavel Clausen. Paul Clancy. Pavel Clausen. Very close….!"

"Now, Kate, don't go being overly dramatic. It could be a coincidence."

Kate sat back and eyed her sister. "In the past few months, we have been seeing too many coincidences to pass up. I think you must be getting hungry."

Betty looked at her watch. "Well, you are right about the

hungry part. Let's go to that little place in Scollay Square. They have the best coffee except for Cook's."

Kate agreed. They picked up their purses, walked out of the office and through the aisles to the front. Miss Baldwin stopped them.

"I do hope this is the end of your questioning. The girls are talking of nothing else. It disrupts their thoughts and their activities." Her voice was sharp.

"I think we have everything we need, Miss Baldwin!" Betty tried to sound soothing. "The next time we come, we will just buy books." She smiled at the older woman, but did not get a return.

Kate grabbed Betty's elbow and waved to Miss Baldwin as she pulled her sister out of the store.

"I think Iris complained," Kate said when they had crossed the busy little street.

Betty looked frazzled. "I don't very often get chided like that."

"Maybe Iris is just really hard to work with. I wouldn't worry about it." Kate didn't let go of Betty's arm until they reached the car. "Let's go have lunch. And then inform Casey about the Claussen last name."

THURSDAY EVENING

It was just before cocktail hour that Casey called. James handed Kate the phone in the foyer and she sat at the little conversation table, smiling.

"Hi, Casey!" she greeted, smoothing her deep blue dinner dress unconsciously.

"I only have a moment, Kate, but I wanted to ask you a question. Remember when Betty said, this morning, that she did not think Paul Clancy was intelligent?"

"I remember," Kate replied cautiously, losing her smile. "Why?"

"Could you get your father to speak to you about high-functioning retarded people getting talked into actions?"

"Do you think that Paul Clancy is retarded?" Kate's eyes opened wide. She hadn't thought of that, seriously. She had thought Betty was being flippant.

"We have talked to him all day, on and off. He isn't responding normally. I think so."

"Well, sure, we will talk to Dad and contact you after dinner. Does that work?"

"Actually, I would really appreciate it if Joe and I could come over and ask him some questions ourselves, after dinner. Would that work?"

"Absolutely. Why don't you two come for dessert, 7?"

"We can do that. See you then, Kate!" Kate hung up the receiver and got up. Betty came down the stairs, headed for their father's study for a cocktail before dinner.

"New development, Betty! Let's talk to Dad." Kate walked ahead of her sister to the open door.

"Dad, I need a favor," Kate announced as she stepped over the threshold as the mantle clock chimed the half hour.

He turned to greet her, martini glass in hand. "Come in, ladies. You are right on time." He handed a glass to each daughter and sat on the leather settee under the window. The two sisters chose matching chairs facing him.

Professor Hadley nestled into a corner of the settee, crossed his legs. "To your latest venture!" he toasted. He sipped his drink, set the glass down and smiled at the two. "What is your need?"

"I need to know how much high-functioning retarded people can follow instructions." Kate presented Casey's idea.

Betty turned in surprise. "What?"

The professor tilted his head. "And where did this come from?"

Kate explained the latest information from Casey and Betty's off-handed comment at Casey's office. "We have a suspicion that there is a relationship between the salesgirl at the bookstore and the kid who got arrested. The kid

76

didn't talk for a long time. But, then, Casey got him to talk this afternoon. The young man is speaking oddly. So, Casey wants to know if he is retarded. And if he is, is he capable of following instructions?"

"That question has no basis, really. Anyone can follow instructions somewhat. If the boy is mentally challenged, there are various degrees of intelligence. If he has been lucky enough to have been raised in a household where everyone else is quite functional, he may have been able to develop enough to be exploitable."

"Exploitable? That sounds so sinister!" Betty responded, furrows showing between her eyebrows.

"My dear, history has always shown that the less intelligent, who can follow instructions, or not, have often been exploited." Hadley reached for his martini and had a sip. "Now, the correct question is, who would have used the young man and what would that person, or persons, be getting out of it?"

"Money?" Kate suggested.

"That is the most common inducement. There are others." Hadley watched his daughters' eyes get smaller as they contemplated alternatives. "Honor, marriage, sex, freedom, position, goods...."

James appeared at the open door and announced, "Dinner, Professor, ladies!"

The three downed whatever was left in their glasses and got up. The two sisters proceeded their father across the hall to the dining room and took their places at the table.

"Dad, I invited Casey and Joe over for dessert in an hour. They are interested in this conversation, too." Kate put her napkin on her lap and smiled over to her father.

"Always good to see those two young men," Hadley nodded happily. "I am glad they are more broad-minded than many of the police officers out there."

It was exactly 7:00 when the doorbell rang. Sally had just finished clearing the table and was putting out the dessert plates. Kate and Betty could hear the young men's voices as they greeted James like an old friend. Kate put her napkin up to her lips to hide a giggle. The two would never get the concept of treating help like, well, help.

Casey appeared first, in his grey suit, tie slightly askew. James had a navy suit on and, although his tie was under control, his auburn hair was not. Hadley stood to greet them and offered them seats, immediately. He sat back down and got right to the reason for their visit.

"My daughters have informed me of the direction your case is taking you. We discussed this before dinner. Here is my opinion: The question is not IF the boy can follow instructions, which, it appears that he can, but WHO gave him those instructions and what inducements did THAT person have to get him to do it."

Sally walked around the table pouring coffee, followed by pumpkin pie with dollops of whipped cream. Joe looked up at her and smiled thankfully.

Casey held up his hand. "Please, sir, before you go on, I have some information that I have yet to share." Hadley nodded an inch and raised his cup in acknowledgement. "I finally got the little guy to say a few words. First, he said he wanted his sister. Iris." Kate's mouth made a big O but nothing came out. "Then he said Cornelius was going to be mad at him."

"Who is Cornelius?" Betty asked, eyes round and unblinking.

"Apparently, Cornelius is a man who wants a very old piece of paper. Paul doesn't know why."

"He actually said Iris' name?" Kate's shocked look was evident.

"Yes, he did."

"It really has to be the same Iris! Too many coincidences," Kate added.

"We are going to go pick her up for questioning in the morning. At her house, before work."

"Why not tonight?" Kate asked.

Casey and Joe laughed. "Kate, it is a matter of a document, not a murder. We have time." Kate lowered her eyes and took a sip from her coffee cup.

"Are you going to pick up this Cornelius, too?" Betty asked.

"We don't have anything about him, yet. No last name, address. Paul didn't know."

"Wait! I know!" Kate burst out. "If this Cornelius knows about an 'old piece of paper', then he has to know Mr. Knapp! How else would he know it exists?" Her eyes started to dance.

"Hold on to that thought, Kate!" Joe instructed. Everyone looked at Joe while he considered his wording of an idea. "Look, this is a long shot, but, it worked when Dr. McGovern lost his Stutz. Only, this time, we don't look in the society pages, we look in announcements."

"What are you talking about, Joe?" Betty looked askance at him.

"I want to put an ad in the paper. "Mr. Knapp's document is secured. The owner may retrieve it by calling... Whatever."

"That is a good idea, Joe," Casey commented. "What would you suggest for a number? I don't think the Sudbury precinct number is a wise choice. Anyone who calls and hears the sergeant answer will hang up."

"They could call here!" Kate piped up. Casey laughed and patted her hand.

"I hardly think that would be a wise choice, my dear. Poor James would hardly know what to say!"

"I know," Joe said, thoughtfully. "Ask the reader to call our apartment number from 8 to midnight, only. We will be there and will handle it." He looked at Casey to get an affirmative response, which was given with a cockeyed grin.

"Call it in to the evening papers first thing tomorrow," Casey instructed.

"What will you do if someone calls?" Betty asked, unsure as to how this would work.

"We really play this by ear," Joe answered. "The idea is to get the person's identification and offer to bring the document to him and arrest him when we get to him."

"Arrest him?" Kate queried.

"Mental abuse of a retarded man, attempted theft, breaking and entering, to name a few." Betty gazed at him in appreciation. He looked at her and smiled.

Kate poked Casey in the ribs and pointed, with her chin, at the pair across the table. He glanced over and winked at her in response.

Discussion turned to plans for the next few days as Sally made another round with her coffee pot. Then Professor Hadley excused himself to go to his study.

"Do you need us for anything tomorrow?" Kate asked the two detectives as the dishes were taken away.

"Yes, as a matter of fact," Casey replied. "I got a message from the curator at the historical society. He wanted to meet with one of us. But we will be spending time talking to Iris tomorrow and I may not have time to get over there. Can you call him back?"

Kate looked wide-eyed at Casey, then Betty, then back to Casey! "Sure, we will! Right, Betty?" Betty nodded vehemently. "We will try to arrange a meeting for this week."

Casey smiled his lopsided grin and pushed back his chair. "So, you take care of that and we will take care of Iris and the newspaper ad. Maybe we will find out something by the weekend."

Joe and the others rose from their seats. It was well after nine. It was time for the two detectives to get ready for the next day.

A little after 9 am, Kate picked up the receiver and dialed the number to the Massachusetts Historical Society. Betty got on the extension. They were passed through to Mr. Benjamin within a minute.

"Good morning, Miss Hadley," Mr. Benjamin greeted. "I am relieved to have one of you return my call." Kate was puzzled by the comment. "Is the document still safe?"

"Oh, of course, Mr. Benjamin. Why are you sounding so concerned?"

"My dear Miss Hadley, it is not every day that I am given the opportunity to handle an extremely rare document that reflects our country's earliest history."

Kate pulled away from the phone and looked at the receiver, surprised.

"So, it is authentic?"

"Yes, young lady. Remember, your detective gave us permission to take a small corner of the document and have it tested. We did so, quickly. It is only a few minutes, really, to do the tests. That is an authentic document from the 1600s. Not quite so fascinating as Governor Winthrop's journal, but just as old."

"It is not a copy of the list?

"Well, we do not have a copy of Nathaniel Eaton's handwriting, but, there was no reason to make a copy of this list of needed items, at a later date. I cannot say with any certitude that he wrote out this list, himself, but, I can say that it was certainly written within a few years of the founding of the Massachusetts Bay Colony, which was 1630, and probably it was written on the date written at the top of the sheet."

Kate wriggled with excitement. "What can we do for you, sir?"

"A number of items need to be addressed. Do you have the owner of record?"

Betty piped in. "It is a little hazy right now. The rightful owner left it in his house when he sold it."

"Ah, yes, I remember that story, now." Mr. Benjamin sighed. "It may have to go to court to separate all the stories. However, it seems to me that the document should be in a safe place. Now, I am not saying that the safe at the police department is not a correct place. But I do believe that the document should be in a museum quality storage unit. These documents are always fragile and need to be kept under glass and not touched." He let out a big sigh, again. "I cannot figure out how it survived so long under such conditions!" The sisters could almost hear him sadly shaking his head.

"Do you want to ask the police for temporary custody of the document until the owner question is sorted out?" Betty asked.

"Ah, Miss Hadley! I, indeed, think that that is the best for the preservation of the paper. Yes, I want to ask. Should I go through Detective Roach?"

"We can ask for you, Mr. Benjamin. We have a way with that detective," Kate offered. She squelched a grin.

"I think that is best, then," Benjamin replied. "I am always available to assist with the handling and transport."

"Thank you, Mr. Benjamin," the two sisters said in unison.

After hanging up, the two called Casey, hoping he was not yet busy with Iris Claussen. The witness had not yet been brought in, so Casey was at his desk.

"So, what did Mr. Benjamin want?"

"He wants temporary custody of the document to put it in a safer environment where it will not get handled or dirtied."

Casey pictured the scenarios of the document sitting in his safe vs sitting in a museum. "I think that would be a wise decision. I will pass it by the captain, then, I will call Benjamin this afternoon. Thanks for handling that call, girls." The sisters could hear a knock on his office door and muffled talking. Then Casey returned to the receiver. "My guest has arrived for a morning of questioning. Talk to you tonight." He hung up before he even heard them say good-bye.

Kate and Betty spent a largely uneventful day, planning a few meals with Cook and passing the early afternoon reading. Finally, the newspaper was delivered at 4 and, rather than wait for the professor to have a first look, the two took the paper apart looking for the ad.

It was a 3 column by 2-inch display ad with black borders, found on page 5 of the evening Globe. It was big enough for anyone to notice, even if it was not in their interest.

Betty looked at the mantle clock in the study. "It is almost 5. The ad says to call between 8 and midnight. I will be so disappointed if this does not work!"

"I will have to stay up til midnight. Casey said he can't call. He wants to leave the line open. Just in case. I promised I would call after the deadline." Kate fidgeted with the papers. "Cocktail time in half an hour. Let's make this paper presentable for Dad, then freshen up."

The cocktail "hour" was 5:30 with dinner at 6, during the school year, a half hour later in the summer. The conversation, as the autumn sun set, was all about the ad in the paper, which had been discussed only after the professor had left the dinner table the night before.

Hadley sat in the corner of his leather settee, with his high-ball on the table to his right. Kate handed him section one of the paper, folded in such a way that page 5 was displayed. Then she took her chair.

"What do you think, Dad? Pretty clever?" Betty asked.

"I think that spending money on ads should be replaced by something more accurate, some day. But this is what we have to work with." He paused long enough for a sip of his drink. "Just enough so that the right person knows this note is for him. Wise move," he added.

"Now we have to see if the fish takes the bait," Kate put in.

"If this person really wants that article, then he will bite. If he is afraid to show his face, he will leave that document alone," Hadley began in his professor's tone. "It depends on why he thinks he should have it."

"How do you mean, Dad?" Betty asked.

"For example, say the person feels that document really belongs to him. He will go after it despite the dangers. But, if he merely wants it and has no thought of previous ownership, he may examine the risk to phoning and decide against it."

"I wonder how many phone calls Casey and Joe will get tonight," mused Kate.

"I am willing to bet that they may get a call or two for several days," the professor commented. "And some of them will be curiosity seekers, only."

The sisters took that under consideration and shrugged as they finished their drinks. They were ready for a change in subject when James announced dinner.

The after-dinner hours were the most difficult, as the two sisters attempted to amuse themselves, waiting for the stroke of midnight. Kate had promised to call Casey. She just needed to keep awake. The two sat in their shared sitting room. But Kate, as much as she enjoyed Agatha Christie, could not concentrate. Nor could Betty with her P.G. Wodehouse. Eventually, they sat and listened to comedians and music on the radio, while watching the clock tick slowly towards the appointed time.

Kate nodded off but was awake at the last stroke of the clock. She jumped up and ran to the phone in her room. She dialed Casey's number.

A groggy Casey answered. "No, dear. We heard from no one tonight. Maybe tomorrow night."

"Oh, dear!" Kate uttered. "I thought maybe..."

"I hoped so, but no. On the other hand, Iris was easy to deal with. She admitted that Paul Clancy was indeed her little brother, Pavel Claussen. She admitted that he was slow and very obedient. Towards anyone. And she admits to giving Paul the book. But that is where it ends. She does not know who this Mr. Knapp is. So, we let Paul go home with her."

"Aren't you going to arrest her for theft of a book?"

Tired as Casey was, he laughed. "No! We do not arrest people for stealing a worn, used book. If the bookstore wanted to press charges, we could. But we have better things to do with the little time we have." He sighed. "We are no further ahead than we were this morning. I hope we get a phone call."

"Did you get the captain to ok the custody transfer to the historical society?" Kate asked.

"Yes. He said he would be glad to get it out of our way. Do you want to call Mr. Benjamin Monday and arrange a transfer? We can get a cop car to move it across town."

Kate smiled and happily stuck out her chest in self-importance. "I would be glad to do that!"

"Look, it's late and I have to go into work in the morning," Casey said. "How about a late afternoon matinee tomorrow?"

"That sounds just right. I would love to see you. Good night, Casey."

SUNDAY AFTERNOON

About 5:30pm, Casey called. Kate was on her way down to Sunday dinner but stopped by her bedside table to answer the phone. She was expecting every call was Casey. Betty stood, leaning against the bedroom door jamb, as Kate answered.

"Kate, we got the call!" Casey's voice was excited.

"Are you sure you should be telling me this police information?" Kate asked, suddenly unsure of her position.

"Kate, if I didn't think you should be privy, I would not have called. Besides, you and Betty have been pretty good about actively participating in this investigation, so I owe you." Kate motioned Betty to come in and listen at the receiver with her. "So, a man called last night. He said he was Mr. Knapp." The sisters opened their eyes wide and looked at each other. "He said he owned the document and it had been stolen from him and he wanted it back."

"Stolen!?" Kate burst out. "Mr. Knapp in the nursing home had it in his house for 50 years!"

"I know," Casey said evenly. "Apparently, this is a family matter that got out of hand. I offered to meet with him tomorrow afternoon and discuss it. He said he would get back to me."

"Humpf! If I was dying to get a document, I wouldn't

hesitate to go to the police once they said they had it." Betty looked at the receiver eyebrows furrowed. She shook her blonde curls in exasperation.

"He will, hopefully, call tonight and arrange a time," Casey added soothingly. "I will keep you informed."

Betty backed away from the phone. "I will tell Dad you are on your way," she whispered to Kate, then left the room.

"I had a very nice time yesterday afternoon," Kate spoke into the phone. Her voice had a purring sound.

"Did you like the movie I chose?"

"It was perfect for getting my mind off theft and on to Jimmy Stewart and you. Thank you, Casey."

"It just came out. I wanted to be the first to see it. All the guys at the precinct have been talking about it."

"So, now you can lord it over them that you saw it already," Kate teased him.

"And I will," Casey added with a chuckle. "Now, let me let you go down to dinner. I know how your father is about punctuality."

"Will you call tonight?"

"After Mr. Knapp calls, how's that?" Kate smiled and acknowledged his promise then hung up to dash down the stairs to the study.

Betty was already seated with the professor but, by a signal, Kate knew that she had not said anything about the phone call. So, as soon as she got to her seat, she announced, "Casey got the phone call for that ad he placed!"

Dr. Hadley raised his eyebrows and stopped short in his reach for his cocktail glass. "What did he get out of the call?"

"It was a man who identified himself as Mr. Knapp. He said the document was his and had been stolen. Apparently, Casey sees it as a family squabble. A very long family squabble." Kate rolled her eyes.

"What happens next?" Betty asked, sitting back for a story.

Kate picked up her glass, took a sip and placed it back on the side table. "This 'Mr. Knapp' may not really be a Mr. Knapp at all. That's what I think. Anyhow, he is supposed to call Casey and arrange to meet and discuss this, this squabble and, maybe, get his possession back."

"I doubt if it will be as simplistic as that, my dear," Dr. Hadley commented. "It sounds like this Mr. Knapp has done some extreme things to get the document, to date. I suspect he is not completely on the up and up."

"How do you think Casey will handle this?" Betty asked, her eyes half-closed as she was picturing the event.

"If you don't mind an old man's opinion….," their father interrupted. "I am sure Lt. Roach knows what he is doing, but this sounds like a little psychological play. Someone should interview that old Mr. Knapp in Jamaica Plain again. Did he ever mention a family squabble?"

Betty sat forward in her seat, looking at her father with interest. "I don't remember such a mention. I can look at my notes, if you want."

Kate thoughtfully swirled her drink. "I don't remember his mentioning anything like that, either. He doesn't seem to have a poor memory, just a poor back. Which is why he sold his house and moved to St. Elizabeth's."

"You might best go talk to him soon, preferably before Casey talks to this 'Mr. Knapp'. Does your Mr. Knapp know about the missing document?"

"He did say that he had some old momentos from years ago," Betty answered her dad.

"Remember, he said that he had a grocery list or something," added Kate.

"He was quite angry about Mr. Patterson not going through everything and the junk man not going through everything. Not sure why he would get upset, though," Betty reminisced.

"He did ask us to let him know if anything happens," Kate pointed out. "I guess we should go over there tomorrow and ask. Before Casey has a chance to talk to this other fellow."

James stepped into the study to announce dinner. The three finished their drinks and left for the dining room to enjoy Cook's fine cuisine.

It was 11:30 before Casey called Kate. She picked up on the first ring so as not to awaken the household.

"He called back, Kate," Casey announced. "We are going to meet tomorrow at the precinct house."

"What time tomorrow?"

"Why? 11:00. Does it matter?"

"Maybe. Betty, Dad and I were discussing the real Mr. Knapp tonight. He never mentioned a family squabble. So, we thought we would go over to talk with him tomorrow. I don't think he is forgetful. But we had better ask, specifically."

"That is a good idea. Can you get the answer before my interview?"

"I think so. We will call as soon as we finish. I'll get Betty to read her notes to you. I can't read her shorthand."

"That may help me organize my interview. Thanks, Kate. Good night! You are the best!"

Kate fell asleep, smiling, with those last words repeating themselves.

MONDAY MORNING

The sisters ate breakfast early, with their father, reviewing the questions they needed to ask the real Mr. Knapp when they got to St. Elizabeth's Nursing Home. Betty called the home and confirmed that Mr. Knapp was available.

It was chilly, according to James. He offered to warm up the roadster while the ladies got their coats. Before 9am, the two were out of the house and in the roadster, headed towards Jamaica Plain.

Twenty-five minutes later, they had arrived at their destination and were sitting with the elderly Mr. Knapp, again.

"I am so sorry that we have to bother you, again, Mr. Knapp," Kate said as soon as they arrived. "But something has happened that we need to clear up."

"Is it about that junk I asked Patterson to deal with?" the old man asked as he settled into his Barcalounger.

"Yes. There has been an arrest in the theft from the church."

"Ah, good. Who is he?" The old man's eyes started to sparkle with interest.

Betty had taken out her notepad and pen. "It is not that easy, sir. The one who was arrested was working for someone and that someone is the one we are after."

The old man shrugged his shoulders. "So, get the guy to tell you who he was working for."

"He did, after a fashion."

"So, go get the guy!" Knapp barked.

"The young man who was arrested said he worked for a man apparently named Mr. Knapp."

The old fellow sat up in his seat and glared at the two ladies, his face turning red. "You are not saying you suspect me, do you? Why would I hire someone to steal my own stuff from me?"

"Oh, no, Mr. Knapp! We don't suspect you at all," Kate objected. "But there is more!" She looked at him pleadingly.

Knapp sat back in his chair and calmed down. "Go ahead," he said.

"We put an ad in the paper after we got a name. He responded. He said it was all about a family squabble. Do you have any clue what that means?"

The old man's eyes reduced to slits as he sat in silence,

meditating about the revelation. The sisters sat quietly, watching his facial expressions change. After 30 seconds, he opened his eyes and looked at the two.

"I'm thinking that must be that old rascal, Cornelius Federman, using my name. He is a distant cousin of mine. Always wanting this and that. He is an idiot. Wants things that are not his, for nothing."

"I don't understand," Kate began.

"Let me explain," the old man interrupted her, poking his arthritic finger at her. "This man and I have a common ancestor. So, we are fifth cousins, or something like that. He wants any artifacts of our ancestor. I don't like him. So, whenever he called me, I would hang up. I don't care for old stuff. It don't mean anything to me. But I sure don't want to give it to him." He leaned forward. "Do you know the danged man sent some retard kid over to my place about a year or so ago and asked to clean up the place? He said he could empty my attic for me. And all for just $10. That Cornelius Federman wants to rob me blind and charge me for it, too!" He sank back into his upholstered seat, breathing heavily.

Betty waited a few moments for his breathing to get calm. Then she looked at him questioningly. "Do you know how much that grocery list is worth, according to the history society?'

Knapp snorted. "Probably $100 more or less. Pricey. I still

97

won't give it to Cornelius."

Betty choked back a chortle. "Sir, I believe the number will be closer to $100,000."

"What?" He almost jumped out of his chair. "You are fooling an old man!"

Kate piped up. "Not at all. We went to the Massachusetts Historical Society last week. The evaluation should be ready this week. They think it is an authentic piece from 1638."

The old man stared at them and eased himself back into his chair. "I'll be damned." He blushed. "Pardon, ladies." He cocked his head, looking at them for an answer before he asked the question. "Who gets that money?"

Betty and Kate looked at each other. "It is undecided. I imagine that it will be divided" Kate sat up looking very serious. "You gave it to Patterson, who didn't want it. He sold it to the junk man, who lost it in a theft. Then someone took it, and put it into a book which was stolen. I think that you would get money, the junk man we paid double what he wanted, so he is not expecting more, and the lady who bought it at the white elephant sale would get some."

Betty nodded. "You may very well get a third, but, we will know more once this goes to court."

"I don't want to go to court. But... did you say a third? Is that a third of $100,000?"

"I am just an investigator, sir. I can't promise anything. But it will be thousands, anyhow."

He rubbed his hands together, gleefully. "I will have out-witted that old Cornelius. What do I got to do?"

"Very little. If the police ask you to identify the man who came to try to clean your house, do so." Betty pulled a calling card out of her purse and wrote her home number on it. "Here," she said, handing Mr. Knapp the card. "This is our phone number. If you need any advice regarding this, you call us." The old man reached for it and nodded.

"We have another appointment, so we need to go," Betty announced, standing up. "I thank you for sharing with us." Kate stood and added her thanks.

"You young girls made my day," Knapp said, happily. "You come right over, again, if you need anything."

"We will do so, sir!" The girls waved and walked out the door.

Kate looked at her watch. It was 10:20. "Let's find a drug store and call Casey. He will want to hear what you wrote before he talks to Cornelius Federman."

They drove over to Egleston Square and found a drugstore a few doors down from the Suffolk deli. Betty parked not too far away. Kate took a nickel from her coin bag, got out of the car and headed in.

There were two phone booths available. She got into one and closed the glass door, inserted her nickel and dialed up the number she knew by heart. Once the desk sergeant forwarded the call, Casey picked up on the second ring.

"Casey, it's Kate! I have some information for you."

"Hi, Kate! I thought Betty was going to read her hieroglyphics to me."

Kate laughed. "No, it was pretty straight forward. Mr. Knapp has a distant relative named Cornelius Federman. He thinks that Federman is using the 'Mr. Knapp' pseudonym."

She could hear his fountain pen scratching on paper. "This is great!"

"Mr. Knapp thinks Federman was behind a young man coming to him a year ago, trying to acquire stuff from the house. And...the young man had funny yellowish eyes."

"So, Paul Clancy was there, at Knapp's?"

"It sure looks like that!" Kate responded. "This Federman has asked for Mr. Knapp's stuff on several occasions. But I guess Mr. Knapp does not like the man. He told us the man asked a few times if he could have the junk."

"So, Knapp has spoken with the fellow a few times?"

"Apparently," Kate responding, nodding. "Does this help?"

"It sure does! Thanks! Now, let me come up with a few questions for this Federman. He will be here in under half an hour."

"I am so glad we could help!" Kate responded. "I'll talk to you tonight!" She hung up the receiver and opened the door. Betty was standing there, with a preoccupied expression.

"Oh! I thought you were going to wait in the car!" Kate smiled at her.

"I had an idea," Betty proclaimed, grabbing Kate by the elbow. "I think we need to go have coffee at Suffolk Deli."

Looking at her sister curiously, Kate allowed herself to be pulled through the drug store and out the door. They turned right and headed towards the deli.

"Do you have another idea boiling over in your brain?" Kate asked as they rushed down the street towards the delicatessen.

"It just hit me." Betty slowed down before getting to the door and turned to face her sister.

Kate stopped her on the busy sidewalk. "What are you

talking about?"

"Remember when we had lunch here and Winnie, the waitress, was talking about Mr. Knapp?"

"Yes. She was talking about his house full of junk..... Wait! We asked ourselves at the time how she knew that. Right?"

"Exactly! And while you were on the phone, I was thinking how I wanted a cup of coffee. And that brought me back to the deli and Winnie. We never did talk about her further, did we? Did you notice that she looks a lot like Iris, over at the bookstore?"

Kate looked at her sister, mouth agap. "Now that you mention it, yes. Tall, blonde. Superficially, at least, they do look alike."

"I am just wondering if there is something there." Betty then added, as she turned to walk into the deli. "Plus, I need a cup of coffee."

They entered and found a booth next to the window. A middle-aged brunette came up to them with pencil and pad. "What can I get for you girls?" She smiled broadly.

"Two coffees, please," Betty ordered. Then she turned to Kate. "Do you need anything else?"

"No. It's too early for lunch, thanks." Kate smiled up at the waitress. "Excuse me, but is Winnie working today?"

"She comes in at 11, honey. Do you want to wait for your order to be taken by her?"

"Oh, no. But can you ask her to come to our table when you see her?" Betty asked. The waitress nodded and went to get the coffees.

Kate leaned as far as she could across the table and whispered, "What do you plan on asking?"

"Does she know Iris Claussen? Has she ever been to Mr. Knapp's before he moved? How messy was it? Does she know Cornelius Federman? Which one first?"

"I would pick the second question as a starter," Kate said as two cups appeared on the table. She looked up to see Winnie. "Hello! Do you have time for a chat before you punch in?"

Winnie glanced at her watch. "Five minutes before I have to punch in."

Kate moved along the bench to make room. "Have a seat." Winnie glanced at Betty who nodded.

"We were talking about old Mr. Knapp last week. And Kate and I were curious if you had ever been to his house."

Winnie looked at Betty with squinted eyes. "Why?"

Betty soothingly smiled. "We are journalists and we are doing an article on why old people go into nursing homes. We know him and we wanted an outside opinion on his reason for leaving his home."

Winnie relaxed and gave them a two-minute description of the state of his home, describing it as the quintessential packrat's haven. Betty, with her ever-present pen and notepad, wrote down what she said. She spoke of potential treasures in the attic and boxes of documents in a back bedroom.

"Do you know Cornelius Federman?" Betty asked, dropping her journalist guise.

Winnie's eyes grew big. "Who are you?"

"Do you know an Iris Claussen?" Kate asked, ignoring Winnie's question. Winnie slid out of the bench, stood, and looked down at the two. Her face was red and her hands were fisted at her sides.

"I don't know who you are, but you can't just come in here asking questions. I won't answer any more." She abruptly turned and walked into the back.

"I think we hit a nerve, here, Kate," Betty said, turning her face away from the retreating waitress. "We should probably tell Casey as soon as we can. I wonder if we have discovered a gang of thieves?"

Kate looked at her watch. "It's after 11. If this Federman is at all prompt, he is probably with Casey. Let's call the desk sergeant and have him give Casey a message."

They left a quarter for their barely touched coffee and left. Walking back to the drugstore, they had to stand in line for a few minutes before one of the phone booths was empty. Kate slipped into the booth, dropped in another nickel and dialed the number. It was picked up on the second ring.

"Sudbury Precinct. Sgt. Ryan speaking," came the booming voice with the slight Irish lilt.

"Sgt. Ryan, this is Katherine Hadley. I need to get a message to Detective Roach right away."

"I am sorry, Miss Hadley, but he is in with a person of interest right now. He asked not to be disturbed."

"But this is about that very client! Please, Sergeant! He needs to know this information now!"

"Ok. Seeing as it's you. Go ahead. I will write it down and get it to him right away."

Kate gave him the short version and thanked him for getting it to Casey immediately. Then she hung up.

The two left the drug store, feeling that they had accomplished something. But the letdown was that they needed to know if they had found any real information.

"That will need to wait until tonight, Kate," Betty told her impetuous sister. "But I am willing to bet that Casey will call you before 9!" She winked. Kate smiled.

MONDAY EVENING

The phone rang during dessert. James brought it into the dining room for Kate's convenience.

"Hello, Kate!" Casey said, excitedly. "Are you and Betty free at 8?"

Kate looked across the table at Betty, pointed to the phone and held up 8 fingers with a questioning look on her face. Betty nodded.

"Yes, we are? Why?" she responded.

"I think we almost have this whole Knapp thing solved. I just need to wrap up a few things. And I could use your help."

"Sure, Casey! What do you need?"

"Can you make an appointment tonight with Mrs. Stevens? She seems a little skittish and I would just as soon have you talk to her. I may have some good news."

"Certainly, we can do that!" Kate reacted happily. "I will have it all arranged by the time you get here! See you then!" She put down the receiver.

"What is that all about?" Professor Hadley asked.

"I think Casey has the case of the misplaced document all wrapped up," Kate responded, smiling at the success. "He is coming over at 8 and wants me to set up an appointment with Mrs. Stevens."

"Marvelous!" Betty beamed approvingly. "I hope that the information that we gave him was of some help."

"He didn't say what worked, but we will know in an hour or so. But, I have to call Mrs. Stevens first."

Two minutes later, Kate got off the phone. She took a sip of her coffee and made a face. "I let it get cold." She smiled at her father and her sister. "We have an appointment to be at Mrs. Stevens' at 8:30. Then, Casey can explain to us all what happened and what is going on."

Professor Hadley scraped the last of his pie off his plate and dabbed his mouth with his napkin. Pushing back his chair, he stood. "I look forward to the report you will inevitably give me in the morning. But this evening's meeting does not need me. I will retire to my study to review the first essays of the semester by my students." He rolled his eyes and his daughters could not help but laugh.

"Enjoy your evening, Dad!" Betty replied as he kissed her cheek goodbye. He winked at Kate as he left the dining room for the rest of the evening.

Sally entered the dining room, as if on cue, to begin her

cleaning.

"Sally, please ask Cook if there is any pie or other desserts available. Our detectives are coming over in an hour," Kate requested.

Sally grinned at them and went to check.

"I do hope this thing is solved," Betty mused. "I also hope that Mr. Benjamin got a sure estimate on that document. It would be nice if Mr. Knapp could have enough money to live someplace a little nicer."

"And if Mrs. Stevens could get a little something for her troubles," added Kate. Betty nodded in agreement. The two retreated to their bedrooms to get jackets for the ride over to the Stevens' house.

Casey and Joe, prompt as ever, rang the bell at 7:59. James let them in and, within a moment, the sisters descended the staircase to greet the young men.

"Did you want a little dessert before we go over?" Kate asked. "It's chocolate cream pie," she added enticingly.

The eyes of the two men lit up. They tended to eat on the run, more often than not, and home cooked desserts were rare. Kate did not need a formal answer. She led them into the dining room, where the table was set for dessert.

"You give Cook my regards," Joe said between mouthfuls,

a minute later. Betty beamed at him.

"Is there anything we should know before we go over?" Kate asked Casey.

"It looks like it may have been a mistake of judgement on the part of Federman. But, that kid, Paul, the slow one, he took on some ideas of his own. But I will tell everyone the story at the same time in a few minutes."

Kate glanced up at the mantle clock. "We promised Mrs. Stevens 8:30. Ten minutes from now." The men finished their pie and coffee and thanked Sally for the extra work.

Mrs. Stevens was in her living room waiting for the four. Joseph served tea as they were getting seated.

"I do hope this is the end of this fiasco!" the older woman nervously pointed out, as she passed around her bone china cups. "It is a fearful thing to worry about your house being broken into. I have had to place additional locks on my doors!" Her smile was shaky. "I haven't heard from you since you arrested that boy in my basement. I assume you have something to add to that evening's horror!" The woman stared at Casey and Joe.

"I thank you for your allowing us to come over and explain to you the situation, Mrs. Stevens," Casey formally began. He picked up his teacup and made a big deal about sipping, putting it down again, and pulling out his always-present notebook from his inside jacket pocket. He then began his discourse.

"As you will remember, the boy had no identification and would only say his name was Paul Clancy." Casey looked at Mrs. Stevens, to make sure she was following. "We questioned him all day on Thursday. Finally, he mentioned "Iris". It just so happened that a lady named Iris was seen with him in a bookstore over a week ago."

Mrs. Stevens eyes grew big. She wiggled excitedly like a child getting into a good ghost story.

"Then he mentioned a person named Cornelius. But not any last name. And then, later, he mentioned a Mr. Knapp. This was a long-shot, but we put an ad in the paper to catch this Mr. Knapp and it worked."

The older woman put her hand to her throat, shocked at the story-line.

"The thing is," Kate interjected. "We had met a Mr. Knapp who, apparently, was the rightful owner of the document. He didn't know its value, though. So, he let go of it."

"Then, we got to meet the man who identified as 'Mr. Knapp' and he turned out to be a man named Cornelius Federman, a distant cousin of the real Mr. Knapp."

"Meantime, Betty and I talked to the Historical Society and Casey showed the curator the document, several times." By now, Mrs. Stevens was looking back and forth from

Casey to Kate, as if she was watching a tennis match. She was almost breathless as she kept turning her head.

"We also did question this Iris, and her sister Winnie. They were all in on helping Cornelius get the document from his cousin. But old man Knapp was a suspicious fellow and once they had been to his house, he wouldn't let them back in to wander through again."

"I should say not!" pipped up the hostess.

"Unprofessional thieves do not act very professionally and they gave themselves away very quickly," Joe added, having been in on the questioning.

"So, what is going to happen to these people?" Mrs. Stevens inquired.

"We can't really jail Paul. I don't think he would understand. He obeyed his sisters and Cornelius. You can't jail someone like that for obedience," Casey answered.

"How about the sisters?" Betty asked. "Will they be accountable?"

"It is all going to the courts, now. Joe and I have to appear at the hearings, but we don't get a vote on the punishment." Casey glanced around. "Personally, I would like them to get 30 days, each. But they are paying to raise their younger siblings, so I am not sure that jail time is the best solution. Their current lifestyles are hard enough."

Casey shook his head.

"What about the document? Is it mine?" Mrs. Stevens asked.

"I think there are several potential owners, here, ma'am," Joe answered. "It will probably be in court for a while so the judges can figure it all out. My bet is that there are two people who have claims. Mr. Knapp, the original owner, and you. Mr. Patterson does not qualify, since he sold it to Stanley, knowing what was in the box. And Kate, here paid Mr. Stanley $10 for the document. So, his bill is satisfied."

"I didn't know I was buying a document!" Mrs. Stevens retorted.

"Yes, but you did pay money for what was in the bag. They may give you a finder's fee, so to speak," Joe explained.

"What I want to know," Betty interrupted. "Was why Paul Clancey, Pavel Claussen, and his sister, Iris, hid the document in an old book.

"We asked her that, too. Paul had lost it for hours when he first stole it from the junk shop. One of his favorite books was *A Christmas Carol,* so, figuring he could identify where the document was would be easy, if he had a large copy of the book. So, she brought him into the store and let him pick out the book. It was an old, colorful book. She thought he would keep it with him long enough to get it over to Federman's the next day."

"But how did it get into my bag?" Mrs. Stevens asked.

"The family goes to that church," Casey answered, leaning forward in his seat to keep Mrs. Stevens' attention. "I don't know why, they live a mile away. But, he was on his way over to Federman's, with the book, and decided to stop into the church. That was the day the finance committee was preparing the bags. People were downstairs wrapping everything in the tissue paper. He came down, put the book down, helped wrap a few things, I imagine. Then left. By the time he got to Federman's, he did not have the book and the document with him. His sister, Iris, questioned him for an hour before she figured it out. They went to the church, but it was already locked for the evening."

"So, we had it the day before the sale?" Kate looked at Casey in surprise.

"I assume that Iris did not know of the sale the next day," Casey continued. "She only told Paul, Pavel, to go back to the church and don't come back without it. So, the poor kid took her command very seriously. I guess he could tell which was the bag with the book, since the book was rather large."

"Of course, when the bag fell and the dish broke, he was confused and ran off. Books don't sound like dishes breaking when they fall," Joe added, smirking.

"So," continued Casey, impressed with his rapt audience. "Paul ran home and told his sister what happened when she got home from work. She knew enough to assume that the document had value. And she sure wanted her cut. So, she sent him back several times to find you, Mrs. Stevens."

The older woman sat back, startled. "So, he did follow me and learned where I live! That's how he broke in….."

Kate put her hand on her hostess' shoulder to reassure her. "I am sure he did it because he was afraid to disappoint his big sister. Not that he is a real thief who wants to break in."

Mrs. Stevens stopped short and looked at her young friend. She relaxed as Kate's reasoning got through to her.

"So, what about that Mr. Knapp? Does he know all this?" She asked.

"He knows much of it. We will let him know more when the courts have ruled. He could use the money. His living accommodations are not at all comfortable." Kate and Betty proceeded to explain the bare bones nursing home environment.

"People live like that?" Mrs. Stevens, having lived more than adequately her whole life, was shocked.

"Yes, ma'am," Joe responded first, remembering how hard it was for his grandparents.

"Well, then," announced the matron. "I will give him any

finder's fee I may receive. I don't need it. My dearest departed husband saw to it that I would lack for nothing, despite the Depression."

"Thank you, Mrs. Stevens," Kate smiled. "He will appreciate that. I'm sure."

"The book goes back to the bookstore, however," Casey added as a last-minute thought. "Iris stole it from there. So, it belongs to the store."

"I understand that, Detective," Mrs. Stevens nodded.

"Do you have any questions I can help you with before we leave?" Casey asked, stretching his legs as he stuffed his notebook back in his jacket.

Mrs. Stevens rose from the couch. "I am so glad you took the time to come and explain this all to me. You four young people are so kind to do that."

"Our pleasure," Betty responded, reaching out and squeezing the matron's hand. "It's late. We had best be going," she added as she, too, rose.

They left and drove back to Louisburg Square. Casey parked in front of the house. He got out and opened the door for Kate. Joe did the same for Betty.

"Kate and I are going to walk a bit," he announced to the others. "It's a beautiful night for a walk with the street lamps shining. And the cool night air!"

Joe just caught Casey's wink in the streetlight. "Good idea!" He slipped Betty's arm around his and walked towards Pinckney St. Casey and Kate walked in the opposite direction, headed towards the Common.

"You must have worked awfully hard, getting those witnesses to give you all the information within such a short period of time," Betty began, trying to break the awkwardness of being alone for the first time. The clicking of her high heels against the slate walk was uncomfortably loud on the quiet residential street.

"Well, we sure could not have concluded it quite so fast if it was not for you two ladies," Joe commented, patting her hand that was wrapped around his arm. "You know, the first time I met you two, I thought you were troublemakers, fun, beautiful troublemakers, though."

Betty glanced up to him, wondering if he was going to mock her. But she couldn't read his eyes with the shadow his fedora cast, so she just had to wait for his next words.

"But I see that we four make a good team," Joe continued. "I will enjoy working with you and Kate again." He smiled down at her.

"Well, thank you, Joe!" Betty returned his smile, moving a little closer to keep warm.

"In the meantime," the detective added. "Do you think we can stop over, every so often, to sample more of your cook's excellent meals? She is much better at food preparation than either Casey or me."

Betty laughed out loud all the way to Cambridge Street.

Elizabeth A Martina is a writer of historical fiction. She hosts a Facebook page, giving tidbits of interest to history fans. She also has a website, elizabethamartina.com, where she comments on writing, travel and her books. Her latest website blogs are discussing our founding mothers, those whom no one has heard of, yet.

Elizabeth likes to travel to places where her stories have occurred. She lived for years in Boston, making it a prime story location. Italy and Virginia are two of her favorite haunts. England is on her bucket list, next.

Quiet is a goal for writers. So, she lives in the mountains with her husband and dog, Hansel, who is not always very accommodating.

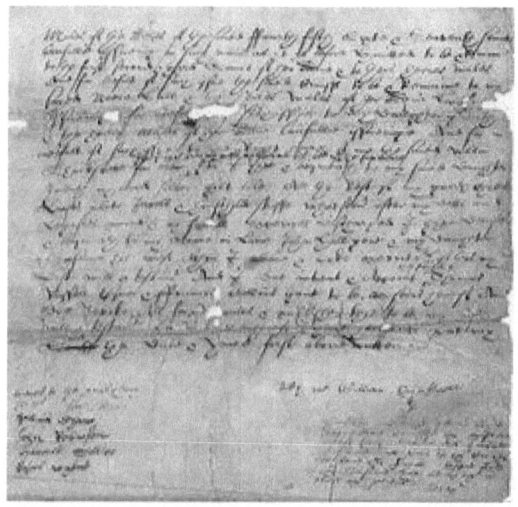

All authors are beholden to their readers for the books bought, appreciated and shared. Please spread the word by putting a review on the Amazon book page for this and all books that you enjoy. The authors will be grateful.